THE ELEVATOR DOORS OPENED TO THE SECOND FLOOR and to . . . well, she wasn't sure what it was at first. The man's smile blinded her. Warm. Welcoming. Amused. And his eyes, a bright laser blue, seemed to be capturing, calculating, and categorizing every atom of her body at once. She was completely undone.

WHAT ARE *LOVESWEPT* ROMANCES?

They are stories of true romance and touching emotion. We believe those two very important ingredients are constants in our highly sensual and very believable stories in the LOVE-SWEPT line. Our goal is to give you, the reader, stories of consistently high quality that may sometimes make you laugh, sometimes make you cry, but are always fresh and creative and contain many delightful surprises within their pages.

Most romance fans read an enormous number of books. Those they truly love, they keep. Others may be traded with friends and soon forgotten. We hope that each LOVESWEPT romance will be a treasure—a "keeper." We will always try to publish

LOVE STORIES YOU'LL NEVER FORGET
BY AUTHORS YOU'LL ALWAYS REMEMBER

The Editors

Loveswept ® 793

GOT IT
BAD

MARY KAY
McCOMAS

BANTAM BOOKS
NEW YORK · TORONTO · LONDON · SYDNEY · AUCKLAND

GOT IT BAD

A Bantam Book / June 1996

ISBN 0-553-44521-9

Published simultaneously in the United States and Canada

*Bantam Books are published by Bantam Books, a division of Bantam Dou-
bleday Dell Publishing Group, Inc. Its trademark, consisting of the words
"Bantam Books" and the portrayal of a rooster, is Registered in U.S. Patent
and Trademark Office and in other countries. Marca Registrada. Bantam
Books, 1540 Broadway, New York, New York 10036.*

PRINTED IN THE UNITED STATES OF AMERICA

OPM   0 9 8 7 6 5 4 3 2 1

Too High Tami and The Whickerchair.
A great story.
A great friendship.
I love you.

AUTHOR'S NOTE

Congratulations on your Thirteenth Anniversary, *Loveswept!*

As it happens, my first *Loveswept* was part of the big Fifth Anniversary Celebration eight years ago. Lord, I was so excited. And so proud to be part of *Loveswept*'s select group of writers: Iris Johansen, Sandra Brown, Helen Mittermeyer, Kay Hooper, Fayrene Preston, Jan Hudson, and the others. . . . I was breathless. And *so* stupid! I didn't even know how to type.

A lot has changed since then. I type, and this is my seventeenth *Loveswept*. I've watched the number of *Loveswept*s on the racks swell from four to six and shrink from six to four again. I've observed a couple of dandy associate publishers stamp their mark on the industry and move on to bigger and better challenges; senior editors have come and gone and editorial assistants have been a biannual treat to meet. My favorite, longtime editor Susan Brailey has had two children. I have four distinctly different types of *Loveswept* covers on my wall. I have failed miserably at fitting my stories into theme months.

I've written a sequel, but never a trilogy. And the biggest change of all is that I am now one of the old-timers!

New blood, new ideas, and new talent keep the *Loveswept* series alive . . . and yet the only unchanged factor in the magic that is *Loveswept* is the unwavering belief in stories that are without formulas or guidelines, in stories that are fresh and innovative and a cut above all the others. Giving writers the freedom to be creative and to use their imaginations is a gift that comes uniquely from *Loveswept*.

It has been a privilege for me to be a part of the *Loveswept* family for so many years. To say that I wish you many more years of continued success is somewhat self-serving, but heartfelt just the same.

Mary Kay McComas

ONE

"Good morning. I'm Dr. McKissack from the CDC. I'd like to see Dr. Kurtsevo Andropov." Her voice was calm but firm as she resisted the urge to reach out and choke the receptionist at Agro-Chem Labs until her pretty hazel eyes bulged. "Please."

Recognition flickered across the young woman's face. "I'm sorry, Dr. McKissack," she said, taking a deep, bracing breath. "Dr. Andropov isn't taking any calls or seeing any visitors right now. If you'd care to leave a message, I'll see that—"

"I am not a visitor," she said, cutting through the standardized rejection speech. She kept her tone soft and mild, the way her mother had taught her. Loud, squeaky wheels got more attention, she used to say, but the quiet ones that kept on moving covered more territory. "I am here as an agent of the United States government and Dr. Andropov will see me. Today. Now."

The receptionist was clearly shaken. Being caught between the United States government and Dr. Andropov was an undesirable position to be in, to be sure.

As the woman began to shake her head the great glass doors to the lobby opened with a swishing noise, and a wiry, highly harried man scurried in.

"Oh, man. Oh, man. I hate this. I really hate this," he told the world as he scanned the lobby and fixed his attention on the receptionist's desk. The small red-and-white cooler he held at arm's length in front of him was marked with a familiar CDC label reading: *Danger. Live Organisms. High Risk.* "I don't mind the body parts, the brains and hearts and stuff . . . and I don't mind most of the bugs," he was saying as he approached them. "The regular kind that can't hurt you, ya know? But I really hate these ones you can't see, the ones that can kill you twice before you even know they're there. Oh, man. Gives me the creeps, I'm tellin' you."

The courier set the cooler on the high rim of the receptionist's desk, swinging his arms wide and taking two giant steps backward.

"Stand back, lady," he said to her. He picked up a black stone that was hanging around his neck on a chain and held it between him and the box—as he might thrust a crucifix at a vampire. "I wouldn't get any closer to that thing than I had to. Oh, man. My girlfriend told me not to get out of bed today. I shoulda listened to her."

Dr. McKissack moved sideways, distancing herself from the messenger rather than his delivery. Even if the box contained the deadly Ebola virus, it was better controlled than the strange young man in the khaki Bio-Transport uniform.

"Good morning, it's . . . Dwayne, right?" the receptionist said, smiling, seeming to take his behavior in stride. Opening a three-ring binder, checking the numbers on the cooler, and shuffling through the pages all at once, she went on, "You're early this morning. Ah, here we go. This one's for Dr. Powhatten. Huh, third one this week," she said, as if it were interesting. "I'll call and make sure she's ready for it."

She picked up the phone and punched in several numbers before her gaze rose and met Dr. McKissack's again. There was a certain resignation in her eyes, and she sighed.

"I'll let him know you're here, Doctor. But that's all I can do."

"Thank you," she said, her soft Southern accent barely detectable. She turned away from the desk when the woman began to speak into the phone. There were court orders to be issued if worse came to worst, she knew, but that would take more time and trouble that she simply couldn't afford at the moment.

Besides, she wasn't what you'd call a by-the-book sort of gal. A big part of an unshakable belief system that she'd developed in her life was that there was an exception to every rule, and every rule was meant to be broken. So, what good was "the book" anyway? As a matter of fact, she so rarely used "the book," she wasn't all that sure what was in it anymore. For the most part, she made up her own rules as she went along, broke them when it was necessary, and made up new ones.

Dr. Andropov's reputation—as brilliant, bullheaded, and badly behaved—extended far beyond the front desk at Agro-Chem Laboratories. She'd been considerably less than graceful in accepting the assignment to investigate his work with a new strain of bacteria called Andropov-B, A-B1 for short, named, no less, after the brilliant Dr. Andropov himself.

Hmmph. Dealing with galactic egos was not her forte. And this particular oversized male ego had pushed her beyond understanding, beyond tolerance, almost to the point of throwing "the book" at him. Actually, any large book would do.

"Upstairs. Bio-Chem labs. Go all the way to the back, all the way down the hall. It's the last door on the left," she heard the receptionist telling Dwayne the messenger.

"Oh, man. I hate this," he said, reaching for the cooler. "I shoulda stayed in bed. Today is not a good day to be messin' with stuff like this. My karma's too weak and my stars are all out of sync and today's Friday the thirteenth. . . . I got a really bad feeling about this," he muttered as he walked toward the elevators. "A *really* bad feeling. I need more protection. What's an obsidian stone against bugs you can't see? I shouldn't even be here. She was right. I shoulda stayed in bed. . . ."

It was a relief to see him swallowed up by the elevator. His anxiety was contagious, she realized, rolling some of the tension from her own shoulders.

She couldn't remember the last good night's sleep she'd had, her mind drifting to the queen-size bed with the cool cotton sheets awaiting her in the apartment she rarely lived in. She traveled constantly; her last real vacation had been two . . . well, certainly no more than five years ago. She rolled her aching shoulders once more. Where had she gone? Her mind went blank. Lord, she couldn't remember her last vacation. It was definitely time for another.

Hearing her name spoken softly into the telephone across the lobby reminded her that she could have avoided this trip—and maybe spent a night or two in that big cool bed, if his royal highness Dr. Kurtsevo Andropov had been so kind as to return her calls. Hmmph. Surgeons were reputed to have serious godlike complexes, but they couldn't hold a candle to a dedicated scientist on a save-the-world mission.

"Dr. McKissack?" She turned to the receptionist but didn't speak. "Dr. Andropov asked me to tell you to please be seated," the young woman said, waving toward a cluster of comfortable-looking chairs aesthetically arranged near a large window displaying a panoramic view of the Arizona desert.

Soft chairs. Scenic locales. The combination always equaled a long, boring wait. She looked back at the young blond woman, who had the grace to look away, ill at ease.

"To please be seated and then what?" she asked.

"He suggested knitting," she said, all but flinching as she prepared herself for an explosion. "And failing that, he said he'd heard there were several hundred different ways to play solitaire."

Maintaining her anger at a low rolling boil was no longer an option in this particular kitchen. The flame flared, her wrath raged and bubbled over the edges. Yet, the only outward sign of this calamity was her white-knuckled grip on the handle of her briefcase as she walked slowly back to the desk.

"Please inform Dr. Andropov that I'll be returning this afternoon with a search-and-seizure warrant," she said softly, her Mississippi drawl thicker and sweeter than usual. "If he chooses not to cooperate, we'll be moving this investigation to Atlanta." She started to leave, then turned back. "Thank you for your trouble."

It was pleasing to hear the frantic ticking of the receptionist's nails at the telephone as she called to warn the doctor. But it was the tiny *tink* of the elevator arriving that went off in her head like the alarm in a fire station.

To hell with this, she decided impulsively, making a U-turn at the doors. This assignment had been foisted upon her because she always got the job done, one way or another. The great Dr. Andropov was not going to be her first failure.

She pressed the button for the second floor—Dwayne the messenger had been directed to the bio-chemistry laboratories there, so it made sense—and already she had a plan in her head.

She was like that. Quick on her feet and planning all the time.

Okay. So she'd bluster her way into the doctor's lab, find out what he was doing, make an evaluation, call it into the office, and go on a long vacation. That was the plan. Oh, and sleep. She nodded. Lots of sleep. She liked it. It was a doable plan.

The elevator doors opened to the second floor and to . . . well, she wasn't sure what it was at first. The man's smile blinded her. Warm. Welcoming. Amused. And his eyes, a bright laser blue, seemed to be capturing, calculating, and categorizing every atom of her body at once. She was completely undone.

"Dr. McKissack," he said, his voice smooth and deep like cool clear water over river gravel. "What a lovely surprise. You're a little smaller than I expected. Prettier too."

She was speechless.

He knew she would be.

"I know, I know. You don't need to say it," he went on. "I'm younger and better looking than *you* expected. I hear it all the time. People are constantly confusing me with my father, who'd be nearly a hundred by now, if he were still alive. You can come out of there. I don't bite."

Naturally, he had an entirely different maneuver for

keeping male bureaucrats unbalanced, but being the humble, unassuming man that he was, it never failed to amaze him how well a more personal approach worked on females.

He was quick to catch the door when it tried to close on her as she took a reluctant step forward—and he was wrong about her confusing him with his father. She knew who he was.

"I, ah, your father . . . He was . . . a visionary." She was stammering like an idiot. She cleared her throat. "I admire his work a great deal. Humankind would have starved to death by now if it weren't for some of the work he did."

He nodded his acknowledgment of her tribute, admired her a bit for having done her homework, and then got to the point.

"But that was him and this is me, and right now you're so mad at me, you can hardly see straight. Am I right?"

She was seeing *very* well. And, unfortunately, she wasn't as mad as she had been. But she still had work to do.

"I don't get mad, Doctor. I do my job. I'm fast and I'm thorough and I try not to interfere with the work in progress. I do, however, very much resent any and all attempts to deny me access to the information I need."

He was smiling again. "Where are you from?"

"You know perfectly well where I'm from," she said, taken back. "Atlanta. The Centers for Disease—"

"No, no. Where did you grow up? Your accent is nearly gone, which is a damn shame, if you don't mind my saying so, but you didn't pick it up in Georgia. It's . . . if you'll excuse the word, baser. More common, less refined. Louisiana? Texas Basin maybe?"

"Mississippi," she said, annoyed that all the speech classes she'd taken hadn't eliminated her drawl completely.

"I thought so. A pretty little Southern belle," he said, looking her over from head to toe—not an altogether difficult task, by the by. She *was* pretty, her stiff neck and prim manner notwithstanding. "And here you are in the dirty world of bacteria and virus. How did you get interested in this field?"

Was he kidding? Did he really believe she couldn't hear the superiority in his voice? The condescension? What was *his* plan? To keep her talking outside his lab until she passed out from fatigue or hunger; or try to charm her to death with his too dazzling smile and pointless prattle, then shove her back into the elevator and out the front door?

Obviously, he had no idea who he was dealing with.

"Dr. Andropov—"

"Call me Kurt."

"Dr. Andropov, my background is such that I am fully qualified to enter your lab and confiscate any organism I feel is a threat to world health. My authority is such that I can have you placed under arrest if you try to detain me. The same is true if you withhold information from me or mislead me with false information. I am perfectly willing to be reasonable with you. I can conduct my investigation in your lab without disrupting your work, but I will be given a free hand here, or this entire affair will be taken to the labs in Atlanta. The choice is yours, Doctor."

"It's not the bacteria," he said, some of the stubbornness and disagreeableness she *had* expected now creeping into his demeanor. "It's an outside influence. The bacteria are benign."

"They can't be that benign, Doctor. We've had to quarantine an entire village in Chad and another in the Ukraine, whose inhabitants were manifesting the same mysterious symptoms. When I left Atlanta yesterday they were sending a team of doctors to the Yucatán to check out several more unexplained deaths due to sudden internal hemorrhaging and renal failure. You and the A-B1 bacteria are the only link to all three places that we've been able to come up with so far," she said, wanting very much to give his work the benefit of the doubt. Absently, she noticed Dwayne the messenger exiting a lab down the hall behind Dr. Andropov. He was still holding the cooler as if it contained raw sewage, and looked more confused and upset than before. "If what you say is true and the bacteria checks out benign, you'll have the satisfaction of knowing that we'll be back to square one with this investigation. If not, then we'll be able to control the bacteria before it does more harm."

"Believe me, sending you back to square one will give me very little satisfaction, Doctor. But I'm telling you, it's not the bacteria." Dwayne was making his way down the hall toward them. "They're a natural part of the nitrogen cycle in the soil, as harmless as those living on the roots of . . . of clover and alfalfa. They produce nitrates for plant proteins, not toxins."

"That remains to be seen, doesn't it, Doctor?" she said. "Particularly, by me. And until I give the A-B1 bacteria a clean bill of health, it will remain under suspicion and unavailable for foreign export. How will Agro-Chem feel about that, I wonder?"

Dwayne, high-strung and ultrasensitive being that *he* was, chose to avoid the tense atmosphere surrounding the two doctors in the hallway and veered toward the laboratory directly behind them, entering unchecked.

"Agro-Chem has nothing to do with this. I'd pull the fertilizer off the market myself if I thought for one second that the A-B1 bacteria in it was potentially dangerous—which it isn't." He reached over and pushed the down button for the elevator, a not-so-subtle hint that it was time for her to leave. He'd been mistaken before; her stiff neck and prim manner added something to her beauty, like bone-dry kindling to the fire burning within her. Her quiet passion appealed to him; tempted him to make it burn hotter. "And please don't think I haven't enjoyed meeting you, Doctor. Perhaps if circumstances were different . . ."

"If circumstances were different, Dr. Andropov, I'd be a man and I'd punch you in the nose for being arrogant and pigheaded," she said quietly. "I find it hard to believe that you're willing to take this kind of risk with hundreds of thousands of lives, for an organism with your name on it. You are conceited beyond words."

"Conceited?"

By hook or by crook she was going to get into his laboratory, and she certainly wasn't above stomping on his pride.

"Well, what would you call someone who names a major agricultural miracle after himself? Humble?"

Only the rigid muscle in his cheek twitched, but he couldn't have distanced himself any further from her if he'd taken a rocket to the moon. She was aware of a frigid breeze blowing through the hallway, and she shivered.

"Actually," he said, "I'd call him hardworking and deserving, but there again we differ in our opinions, Dr. McKissack. And since we appear to be unable to agree on anything, perhaps now would be a good time for you to

run along and get your court order, and for me to return
to my work."

He turned his back on her. Dismissed her. As if she
were a . . . ah, a . . . While her mind sputtered for
the proper term, her temper was throwing sparks everywhere.

"Don't even *think* of ignoring me, Dr. Andropov,"
she said, stepping quickly to place herself between him
and his precious laboratory. "This is not a child's game
we're playing. People are dying. I don't have time to
stroke your ego or smooth your ruffled feathers. And I'm
not leaving this building until I have the information I
came for, so you might as well cooperate with me."

She was almost as startled as he was to find her face in
his. His eyes, two or three inches higher than hers, were
staring at her with wonder and . . . and something
else. . . . Why didn't she simply go for the court order,
take the entire mess to Atlanta, and save herself a ton of
trouble? she speculated, almost as if she were reading his
thoughts. Two or three inches higher—a mere nod of his
head, a slight stretch of her spine—and their lips would
touch, she continued to speculate; almost as if she were
reading his thoughts.

"I'm sorry," she said, quickly stepping away, her back
against the door to his lab. Her face was burning hot, but
she knew she wasn't blushing—she never blushed. Her
mother used to try to teach her to blush by holding her
breath, saying it was an entirely feminine thing to do and
that it could prove to be handy in any number of awkward situations, but she never did get the hang of it. "I
have to insist that you take me seriously, Dr. Andropov.
Getting court orders and policemen and shipping everything to Atlanta is time-consuming. And while we're did-
dling around here with all that"—she flung her arms out

wide—"more and more people are being infected. Please." She could see her new tactic was getting to him. "Please. I promise I won't get in your way. Just loan me a microscope, and you won't even know I'm there."

Was she serious? She smelled like sunshine. She was blushing like a schoolgirl. How could he not notice her?

"My dear Dr. McKissack," he said, and that's when she noticed the smattering of gray hair at his temples. Silver and black—always a tasteful, elegant combination according to her mother. "My laboratory is more my home than the house I own, and I guard it against all intruders. I'm sure you'd be very neat and tidy and quiet as a little mouse, but believe me, I would know you were there."

"All right," she said, her brow furrowing thoughtfully. She'd dealt with eccentric scientists before, she could figure out a compromise with this one too. You treat them as if they were spoiled rotten children, make them think they're getting whatever they want, and then take what you need from them. "What if I work with your lab assistant? Ask him the questions. Get the data and slides from him. I don't need much room, any empty office space would do. You wouldn't have to talk to me or look at me or—"

"Talking to you and looking at you are not what I'm objecting to," he said, moving to stand beside her at the door. Her heart stopped. His hand slid behind her to the doorknob. An army of goose bumps marched across her. "If that were all you wanted from me, I'd be delighted to cooperate with you. Eager, even," he said, lowering his face to hers, tearing nearly every thought in her head to shreds with the look in his eyes. For a world-shattering millisecond or two she was positive he was going to kiss her, and, of course, she was vaguely conscious that he was being sexist and totally unprofessional. She was struggling—hard—to be angry and indignant when he murmured, "Unfortunately, you want more. I work alone, and my lab's off-limits. Excuse me."

No kiss?

"No." She stretched her arms wide. Pushing Kurt away from the door, she plastered herself to the wood behind her. "Think about what you're doing, Doctor. If I have to come back here with a warrant, the CDC will take everything. You'll have no control—"

She screamed when the door suddenly flew open behind her and she went falling backward into Dwayne and his red-and-white cooler. She knocked her head against it on the way to the floor, landed on her backside, and lay watching the stars on the back of her eyelids for several long seconds.

"Oh, man. Oh, man. This is it. I knew it," she heard Dwayne whining. "I'm covered with 'em. You're covered with 'em. They're in the air. We're all gonna die. I need a cigarette."

"Dr. McKissack? Doctor?" Kurt had her hand in his and a palm to her cheek. "Are you all right? She hit her head," he said to someone—probably not Dwayne, as he was still moaning on and on.

"Why me? Why today? Why didn't I listen to her and stay in bed?" Dwayne wailed.

She opened her eyes. Her eyeballs hurt, and the back of her head ached as well. She made an effort to sit up and felt strong arms assisting her.

"That was quite a fall," Kurt said, speaking very near her ear as his fingers lightly explored the back of her head for a lesion. "Are you all right? Are you dizzy? Blurry vision?"

"I'm okay," she said. If he were straddling her body

with his, she wouldn't have been more conscious of it, or less self-conscious. Every nerve in her body was jumping with excitement.

"Would you get her some water, Joanne?" he asked the girl leaning over them. She was dressed in jeans and a lab coat and appeared to belong there—like the assistant he said he didn't have.

"No way, man. You're not okay, lady. You're definitely not okay," Dwayne was saying as the girl disappeared behind another door. "If anything's broken inside this cooler, you are very not okay. You're *crawling* with invisible killer bugs. Larry, my boss . . . the dispatcher? He warned me all about this. We'll have to seal off this whole floor and call in—"

"Whoa. Whoa. Whoa." The doctor all but dropped her back on the floor when it became apparent that Dwayne needed him more than she did. "Let's not be hasty now. We don't know that anything's broken. We don't even know what's in there. Let's—"

"Invisible killer bugs," Dwayne told him.

"Well, let's not panic, then," Kurt said calmly. "Let's just take it real easy. We'll close this door." He stepped over her to close the door to the hall. "Let's just peek inside and see what's happened, shall we? You know, they pack these things pretty securely for transport." He took the cooler from the courier's outstretched hands as if it were a live bomb. "You could probably drop it down an elevator shaft and not break anything."

"Not today, man. My karma's weak and my stars are all out of sync and it's Friday the thirteenth. We're gonna die."

Kurt stared at him in fascinated horror, as if he were crawling with *visible* killer bugs.

"We're *not* going to die," he said. "Dr. McKissack is

too young and too pretty to die. Isn't that right, Doctor?"

She was getting a full-blown headache.

He set the cooler on a nearby desk, situated just inside the door, and started to open it.

"No. Wait, man," Dwayne said with both hands in the air. "My old lady has this hang-up about me taking responsibility. She says that's why I came back this time, you know, to live my life over again? Because I need to learn how to take responsibility. That's why she got me this job with her brother, Larry. So I could learn responsibility." He hesitated. "I guess maybe *I* should open that and check it out. I'm supposed to be responsible for it till it gets to the right person." His expression brightened. "Is one of you Dr. Powhatten?"

The two doctors looked to each other and then back at Dwayne before they shook their heads.

"Oh, man. I hate this. I really do," he said, approaching the cooler with undiluted dread. "I really need a cigarette."

"Let me open it. I do it all the time. It's no big deal. She didn't hit her head on it all that hard. It'll be okay. You'll see," Kurt tried to reassure him.

"Thanks, man, but no. I gotta do it. I'm responsible. And once I learn to be responsible, I get to have babies and learn nurturing," he said. Then, as if there were an echo in the room and his words had come bouncing back at him, he realized how weird that sounded. "Next time I live, that is," he said. "I'll probably be a woman, have babies and learn to nurture. Not this time."

The control in Dr. Andropov's expression was astounding. He was either holding back laughter or rage, but it was impossible for her to tell which.

Gingerly, Dwayne pressed the button on the side of

the cooler and slowly started to push the top over the rim of the box. He jumped three feet back, holding his heart, when Joanne returned, holding a glass of water.

"Oh, man!" he wailed, pale as her lab coat, sweat beading on his forehead. He held his heart in place a few more seconds, then took the water, drank it, handed the empty glass back, and thanked her politely.

It was time to get up off the floor and, if Dwayne didn't act responsibly within the next minute or so, open the cooler herself. *She* still had a job to do. And now she was going to have to do it with a headache.

He did it with his eyes closed, pushing the lid back slowly, slowly, until it locked itself in an open position. Then he stood there, squeezing his lids tight, refusing to look inside.

With an impatient noise her mother never approved of, she stepped forward to peer over Dwayne's shoulder at five glass vials nestled firmly in Styrofoam at the bottom of the box. Though he didn't come close to touching her, she could feel Dr. Andropov too close behind her, looking at the same thing over *her* shoulder. The tips of her fingers started to tingle.

"Do you mind?" she asked, turning her face to his.

He didn't at all. She had the nicest green eyes he'd ever seen. Soft, dreamy eyes . . . with an attitude. He rather liked the way she smelled and the warm sensation of standing close to her—but he stepped back anyway.

"There, you see," he said brightly. "Nothing's broken. Now you can all leave."

"I thought you said you didn't have a lab assistant," she said, turning on him.

His eyes darted to Joanne, then back again. "No, I didn't. I said I work alone. And I do."

"Then what do you call her?" She pointed an accusing finger at Joanne, who was, by now, stupefied by the whole situation.

"I call her Joanne, of course."

Her eyes narrowed and one hand came slowly to her hip. She was about to tear his lungs out and hand them to him when Dwayne interrupted.

"We don't know that, man._ These little bottles could be cracked, man," he said, turning with the vials—Styrofoam and all—in the palms of his hands. "Those bugs could be crawlin' through the cracks right now, and we wouldn't know it. They could be—"

She growled. "For crying out loud," she said, her cultured tones slipping into her father's longshoreman style. "How long have you had this job?"

"Three months," he said, watching her reach inside the cooler to withdraw a fistful of papers.

"Well, you might want to consider *re*considering this career choice," she said as she scanned the invoices: *Salmonella enteritidis*, nasty stuff, but they'd have to ingest it; *Vibrio cholerae*, cholera, untreated, it could kill you in twenty-four hours; *Neisseria meningitidis*, meningococcal meningitis, she wouldn't want to be infected with it but it was ninety-two percent curable; *Yersinia pestis*, the Great Pestilence, Black Death, bubonic plague . . . and *Bilborre essidea*, worse than anything God ever created, it was man-made and absolutely lethal. "Ah—um . . . I say we put the vials back in the container, close it up, and call in a disposal crew, just in case the vials are cracked," she said, blindly handing the invoices to Kurt. Impatience was suddenly no longer the emotion *du jour*. In Dwayne's place she might be a little leery herself. "I doubt they've contaminated anything yet and they don't appear to be leaking, so we're safe enough, I think."

"You think?" The panic in Dwayne's voice was high and shrill.

"She's positive, aren't you, Doctor?" Kurt said, wedging his body between her and the vials in the messenger's hands. Perhaps it wasn't the most appropriate time to notice how wide his shoulders were or that he had a clean smooth hairline along the nape of his neck; that the collar of his lab coat was bright white and pressed with starch; that his dark hair was full and thick and healthy looking, or that he smelled like a combination of soap and his own personal musk—but there it was, in front of her nose. "And so am I. Absolutely positive," he said. "As long as the vials aren't leaking, we're perfectly safe."

If she believed in such things—and she didn't—his confident words could have been construed as an insult, a challenge, a dare to the gods of Friday the thirteenth. Or so it might have seemed, if one believed . . .

At that moment a small gray-haired woman burst into the room, bumping into Dwayne, who, in his panicked state, threw the vials into the air toward Kurt, who caught them, dislodging the top half of the Styrofoam container. In his frantic effort to keep the specimens intact, he fumbled for the top half of the container with one hand and rattled the vials precariously in the other until he lurched in a final effort to retrieve the top, sending the vials flying in her direction. Knowing she'd never catch all five vials, she dropped her briefcase and threw herself backward to avoid them. Unbalanced, she fell again, landing on her bottom, just in time to watch each vial—as if in slow motion—hit the floor, shatter, and scatter its contents everywhere.

TWO

Silence was like a physical presence as the five of them stared in horror at the broken vials. Every second became a lifetime as they stood like statues waiting for Death to make his move.

Afraid to breathe, her body trembling with each pounding heartbeat, she slowly raised her gaze to the others, meeting Kurt's eyes straight on. He looked back at her with a blank expression, as shocked as she was.

Though she didn't see him move, it was the entirely responsible Dwayne who broke the spell of terror by smashing the glass rod in the fire alarm.

The intense noise of the alarms had her on her feet, inspecting her body for obvious signs of contamination. "Oh God. Oh no," she began to chant over and over. The gray-haired lady stepped forward to help, muttering something unintelligible. In fact, *everyone* was talking and shouting, but all she could hear was her own pathetic little prayer.

"Oh, man," Dwayne wailed, his arms flailing in the

air. "I know what to do. I know what to do. I read this part twice in the manual. Nobody move!"

Too late. Joanne was urgently talking to someone on the phone. Kurt had left the room and was returning with a large black rubber apron that he carefully placed over as many broken vials and their contents as possible.

"Okay. First we notify emergency services. Then we contain the contaminant," Dwayne announced, again too late.

Feeling strangely detached from the others, she felt numb all over. She had no sensation in her fingertips. She was calmly considering the possibility of this numbness being the first symptom of exposure to any of the five deadly organisms, when Dr. Andropov stepped into her narrow line of vision and said something that sounded remarkably like, "Give you a bath."

He grabbed her limp arm and started pulling her toward the door Joanne had used earlier—his office, she suspected, as the anteroom they were in appeared to be a reception area. Vinyl-covered chairs. End table. Bare walls. Desk. Files. Nearly dead potted plant. Your basic unfriendly, unwelcoming decor, she thought, being totally objective in her assessment.

Dwayne was calling for, "Step two. Sterilization. Okay, okay. That's disinfectant showers and antibiotics for us; bactericidal detergent to everything else. Does anybody have a cigarette?" as they left the small room and entered Dr. Andropov's sanctum sanctorum.

She was immediately aware of the slight increase in heat and humidity and the smell of damp soil. A door leading to the laboratory stood open, and she was not at all surprised to see the steamy glass windows of a greenhouse at the far end of the long narrow room. What would a botanical biochemist do without one?

If it wasn't so childish and so typical of him to think of his laboratory as hallowed territory, the birthplace of miracles, she might have mentioned to him that it looked exactly like a thousand other labs she'd seen, with its bottles and tubes and microscopes and autoclaves and chromatograph and . . . stuff. She might have told him it was smaller than most too—but she wasn't a mean-spirited person.

"They'll give you two red bags. Put your watch and jewelry in one and your clothes and the towel in the other," she heard him say quite clearly. *Red* plastic bags denoted contaminated material. She turned her head in time to watch him open another door to a closet-sized rest room, reach in, pull out a towel, and jam it into her hand—the hand he still held by the wrist. "They'll autoclave what they can and return it to you later, but the rest will have to be destroyed."

"Destroyed?" She knew what that meant; knew why it had to be, but in her mind the connection shorted out.

"Burned," he said. He noticed the open door to his laboratory and swung it closed immediately. That left only the cream-colored walls scattered with diplomas and photographs, dark well-worn mahogany furniture, a mini-library, a few personal mementos, and *him* to look at. "Try to remember if you have copies of everything in your briefcase, what personal items you want removed"—he handed her two plastic-wrapped Betadine brushes used for sterilizing skin—"they'll want to burn that too. Scrub everywhere. Your hair, between your toes . . . everywhere, whether it came in direct contact or not, understand?"

"Of course I understand," she said, wrenching her wrist from his grasp. The man had gall, telling her how to bathe.

He stopped short and stared at her as if he hadn't realized she was there; and maybe he hadn't, in a way. Until she distracted him by pulling away, he'd been operating automatically.

It was that look she'd given him as she'd sat helpless on the floor, staring back at him in stark horror, her pretty green eyes clouding with abject despair. Complete hopelessness. That's what set him off, threw him into a tailspin. He liked her feisty. In a strange, shock-contorted moment he visualized his world becoming a dreary place without her spunk and spirit and . . . well, he went a little nuts for a second.

An overreaction. It could happen to anyone, he consoled himself. *She* was a pain in the butt. The boy was a messenger from hell. Joanne and Polly Powhatten were . . . Ah, hell. They were all in his way now. Nothing but trouble.

"You know the routine, then," he said to her, his tone brusque. "The contamination crew should be here by now. You'd better get started. Shower's there"—he pointed into the dark closet—"and there are more towels in the cupboard if you need them. They'll want you to stay inside to bag out and—"

"I know, Doctor. Isolation techniques are pretty basic," she said, suddenly vexed. Stiff with an unreasonable anger, she marched to the designated door, swishing the towel in her hand with pent-up frustration. It was a tiny room. Sink, built-in cupboards, commode, and shower—hardly enough room to turn around in.

Great. She turned on the light and slammed the door closed behind her. No bed. No sleep. No vacation. While she waited to turn black and die, she was going to be imprisoned with an ornery egotistical scientist, an insane deliveryman, and two women she didn't know from Adam . . . or Eve. Just great.

"Hey," she called, opening the door enough to stick her head out and watch him turn around. "How long is the incubation period? A couple of those specimens are twenty-four hours, I know, but—"

"*Bilhorre essidea* is ten to fourteen days," he said flatly, his expression that of someone who was being massively put upon.

"Two weeks?" She could barely whisper the words.

"I see you're into equivalents, Doctor. That is correct. Two weeks. Two weeks of fun-filled confinement, here, in my laboratory. You should be careful what you wish for," he said, before leaving her without a backward glance.

"Two weeks?"

She closed the door softly this time and started to undress. Two weeks? Isolation was not a new concept to her, but always before she'd been free to move in and out of isolated areas, gowning up with masks and gloves, observing sterile techniques. It was nothing. A minor inconvenience. Part of the job. But *being* isolated? For two weeks? Wondering every second if you were going to live or die?

Two weeks? Not much time. There was still so much she wanted to do.

She used hot-hot water and scrubbed as hard as she could with the Betadine brushes, onc in each hand, deluding herself with the idea that if she were clean enough, she'd live—maybe even shorten her period of confinement.

"Dr. McKissack?" she heard through the spray of the water. Someone was in the room with her. "Dr. McKissack. Don't be alarmed," the person said when she peered around the shower curtain at him, yellow-orange soap and froth clinging to her as if she were something rabid. He was no less frightening dressed in a bright yellow moon suit, a protective decontamination outfit with its own air supply, and a small clear plastic window in the helmet for him to see out of. He filled the entire closetlike space. She felt not only naked and diseased, but crowded, as she stared at him dumbly. "Emergency services, ma'am." He turned slightly to face the wall. "We've set up Dr. Andropov's lab as a sterile unit. When you're finished, put these on"—he tossed blue surgical scrubs onto the lid of the commode—"and knock twice on this outer door. We'll red-bag and sterilize this unit before the next person comes in. Any questions?"

"How, ah, how long?" She knew, but she needed to hear it again.

"Ten to fourteen days, ma'am," he said shortly. "Longer, of course, if it turns out you're a carrier without symptoms. We'll have to test you for that before we can let you go. There's a phone in the lab, you can call your family, ma'am. We'll have meals brought in, beds, games, books, whatever you need. A physician's been called, and there's a medical facility on standby in case . . . Well, just in case. We'll try to make this as easy on you as we can, ma'am."

"Thanks. I, oh, wait. I have things at my hotel. A suitcase. Can someone pick it up for me, and check me out of the hotel?" she asked, proud of her practical thinking. Her mother would have been impressed.

"Yes, ma'am. I'll see what I can do," he said, backing out the door as if suddenly uncomfortable with her state of undress.

"Thanks," she said, closing the curtain, realizing it was opaque but hid very little.

Stupid. Who cared if someone saw her naked? She could be dead in two days or a week. She could run through Dr. Andropov's lab naked every day until she died, and who'd really care?

She closed her eyes and took a deep, calming breath. This was, and would continue to be, one of those situations her mother used to talk about; one she would need to rise above; take control of; make the best of.

She braced her hands against the wall, then lowered her forehead between them. What did her mother know about her life? Hot water streamed across her neck and shoulders and down her back, rinsing away the yellow Betadine foam. She needed to scream, hard and long. A soul-piercing howl would feel so good. . . .

She turned the water off, dried herself, and put on the blue pajama-type garb she'd been given. She wouldn't scream. And she wouldn't consider dying either—she simply didn't have the time to die. Combing her hair with her fingers, she looked in the mirror over the sink and cringed at her new drowned-rat look. On second thought, there was a good chance that she might *have* to scream eventually—but she definitely wasn't going to die with her hair plastered flat to her head, and that was final.

The door swung open when she gave the signal, and the man in the bright yellow moon suit handed her a pair of paper booties that were normally worn over shoes, but in this case went directly on her feet.

Then, suddenly, she was in Dr. Andropov's laboratory.

Alone.

Ah, temptation.

Every moment of resistance to temptation is a victory. That was Dryden . . . no, those were Faber's sage words. *The absence of temptation is the absence of virtue;* Goethe, for sure. And Spurgeon—her mother's favorite—was, *Some temptations come to the industrious, but all temptations attack the idle.*

Her mother knew a thousand quotes and a million reasons to resist temptation, but had she ever found herself alone in Dr. Andropov's lab?

Heck, no.

I see the devil's hook, and yet cannot help nibbling at his bait. Moses Adams was a little more human than most pundits, she reflected as she wandered farther into the room.

Her hands were clasped tightly behind her back, but she couldn't keep her eyes closed without bumping into things. And it couldn't be a sin to accidently *see* something lying out on a countertop, or to read a file cover here and there.

She bent over an unlit microscope and saw nothing. *Better shun the bait than struggle in the net.* Now, *that* was Dryden, she recalled, resisting the urge to turn the microscope on. There was already a slide in place. Two seconds only. Just on and then off again.

No degree of temptation justifies any degree of sin—Willis.

She sighed and regretfully conceded that she couldn't bring herself to snoop through Dr. Andropov's work without his permission. Some things truly were sacred, and the workings of a brilliant mind were a prime example.

She continued to wander through the small lab, one of a hundred or more belonging to Agro-Chem Industries, a diversified company that was involved with everything from pesticides to chick hatching. Nothing was in progress. No chemical analysis on the chromatograph.

The computer was displaying a bright-colored screen-saver pattern. No printout on the fax machine. The refrigeratorlike incubator most certainly contained breeding cultures, but she thought better of opening the door to make sure.

By the time she reached the glass door to the green-house, she was sick to death of being good and virtuous. She pushed her way in without the slightest twinge of guilt. She hadn't noticed the color of Dr. Andropov's thumbs before, but clearly one of them was deeply green. The warm, humid room contained a . . . a plethora of lush plants, some blooming.

It was really quite beautiful.

Peaceful.

Almost . . . serene.

She came across a large portable planting trough, an experiment in progress, with perhaps two hundred or more small green plastic starter pots lined up in rows of trays. All were at various stages of growth. They were marked either *rice* or *wheat*. Soil samples varied in color and consistency. All were neatly labeled by site number and country—*17 Honduras; 44 Saskatchewan; 84 Burma; 24 Nigeria.* The growth in weeks was noted, also genera-tion and lot number. She recognized some of the older plants. Gaines wheat with its thick stalk and heavy heads of grain, and IR-8—the miracle rice.

"If I'd taken the time to shave after my shower, you'd have everything figured out by now, right?" Kurt asked from the doorway.

She'd been expecting him—her best reason for re-sisting the temptations of his laboratory. She knew he wouldn't leave her alone there for long. She also knew he wouldn't take the time to shave—couldn't, as chancing a nick in his skin, his body's natural barrier to disease, would have been terribly foolish. And foolish he wasn't. Still, she hadn't expected him quite so soon. She wasn't as prepared as she would have liked for Round Two.

"Actually, I thought I'd have more time, Doctor," she said, turning to him, her hands still locked behind her back. "Did you scrub everywhere? Your hair and between your toes? If even one of us is still contaminated, the rest of us are at risk."

"I, too, know how to take a shower, Doctor." He was watching her with his cool blue stare. With her brown hair slicked back, her eyes looked bigger and brighter than before, her cheekbones more pronounced. She looked small—petite—in the blue scrubs. Strange the way her business suit made her look taller and tougher, he thought. "Of course, I'd be willing to take another if you feel the need to supervise me—to be absolutely sure I didn't miss anything, that is."

The tiniest movement around her eyes was the only sign that he'd annoyed her. He sensed she was constantly on the verge of blowing a gasket, and yet she gave so few outward signs of her anger. It fascinated him—he, who exploded at the drop of a hat, who could no more conceal his emotions than he could a cat at a Doberman convention.

"I'll take your word for it, Doctor," she said, her cheeks burning once again. She ignored it. "I suppose we need to start trusting each other sometime."

"Is that my cue to offer to show you my work to date with the A-B1 bacteria, Doctor?"

"It could be," she said. She had hoped it would be. "Or we could call it the first step to a truce."

"A truce," he said, and he smiled. "I hadn't realized we were at war, Doctor."

"No, no. Not war. Just . . . at odds, I'd say," she

said, walking slowly toward him, her paper shoes scuffing lightly across the floor. She definitely liked his looks. Too bad he was such a poop. What a shame it would be if he'd washed away that well-scrubbed musk smell he'd had earlier. . . . "We both want the same thing, don't we?"

He hesitated. He knew what she wanted, but if she had any idea what he wanted just then . . . well, maybe she'd forget about what she wanted and they *would* both want the same thing.

Nah. She wasn't the type. Wasn't his type. Too all-business and no fun. Too much like his ex-wife.

"In a broad sense, I suppose we do," he said. "Broad meaning that we're working toward the same results from different fields of endeavor. In which case, if you stick to your field and leave me to mine, I believe this truce of yours will work out nicely."

He hadn't said anything deliberately insulting to her, and yet once again he got the impression she was about to burst like an unpunctured potato in a microwave.

"You're not being reasonable, Doctor. We're both biochemists. And there's not that much difference between microbiology and micropathology. In fact, our two chosen fields are closely related. Life and death." She grinned, and knew she was appealing. You see, her smile was the only thing her mother never tried to improve on. "I can walk the walk and talk the talk of microbiology," she said, trying to entice him. "In college I had friends who thought I was a pretty good sounding board when they were stumped and . . . and I can keep secrets like no one you ever knew before."

His anger was instantaneous and startling.

"You went too far, Doctor," he said, opening the door to leave. "I was almost convinced. I almost believed you. But you went too far. I'm fairly certain that it's genetically impossible for a woman to keep a secret."

"Oh, now, wait a second," she said to the closing door. She hurried to catch up with him. "If you want to get genetic about this . . ."

They were no longer alone.

"Oh, man. I can't believe this," Dwayne was saying, standing just outside the office door, looking particularly stupid in the too-short scrub blues he'd been given. "My old lady is never going to believe this. I'll probably lose my job. I'll never be responsible. Oh, man. I'd better call her. The guy in the suit said there was a phone in here."

She automatically pointed to it, remembering where it was. Kurt noticed her familiarity with his laboratory and glowered at her. She raised her brows and shrugged innocently. Could she help it if she was naturally observant?

"Do you guys smoke? I left mine in the van." They shook their heads. "Oh, man. Hi, it's me. You'll never guess what just happened. . . ."

"Is it me, Doctor, or women in general you hate?" she asked, continuing their conversation in a hushed tone of voice. "If it's me, I apologize for any indiscretion I may have committed. But if it's women in general, I feel I should advise you to get over it. We constitute half the population of the world, and it isn't always going to be possible for you to work solely with men."

He gave her a steady look, almost as if he were reevaluating her in some favorable fashion, then he turned and started to walk away. "I don't hate women. I hate intruders. Female intruders are particularly irksome, as they don't seem to know when to give up." He gave her a pointed look over his shoulder as he sat down in front of his computer.

The bone of contention between them was clearly above his ears, she decided, smoldering. There was no reasoning with a man who was so narrow-minded that he could look through a keyhole with both eyes. Still, she wasn't about to give up.

She was in his lab, after all, for the next fourteen days and fourteen nights . . . if she didn't die.

She paced the small aisle between the end of the work counter and the glass wall of the greenhouse, listening to Dwayne as he explained to his girlfriend what happened, with amazing accuracy.

"Man, it was like a slow-motion nightmare that lasted ten years. Bugs everywhere, but you couldn't see 'em. You just knew they were there, crawlin' around. What? Yes. I was totally responsible. It was all my fault. Sure, but doesn't taking all the credit for it count? I even told the guy in the suit it was my fault. His suit? It's yellow. . . . Oh, man. How come you didn't tell me you saw a man in a yellow suit in my cards last night? . . . You thought it was the guy in the chicken suit at Chick-O-Fillet?"

The headache she had before the . . . the "slow-motion nightmare that lasted ten years" was back with a vengeance.

Joanne had finished her shower and, after several minutes of looking about as if she were lost, had taken to a straight-backed chair near the door leading to the outer office. She was very young and pretty, but her quiet demeanor made her seem rather mousy—a manner her own mother would have had a field day with, she mused.

"My, oh, my my me," the older woman, Dr. Powhatten, said, emerging from Kurt's office in her blue pajamas, her permed gray hair wet and matted. "Such a hoo-ha they're making. Goodness, you'd think we'd never been exposed to bacteria before."

No one responded.

"And, of course, that's ridiculous. We're exposed every day, in every way." She laughed. "Well, hey!" she added. "What a day."

She had everyone's attention by then—including Dwayne's—but no one knew what to say.

"Well, no sense fretting about it. Nothing to be done. We'll just have to make the best of it." Would a primal scream relieve a headache? "My late husband, Andrew, used to say there was nothing like a small disaster for bringing people together. And here we are . . . together."

She stared back at each of them in turn.

"Of course, dear Joanne and Kurt and I already know one another, but perhaps we should just go around the room and introduce ourselves."

There was one in every crowd—a self-appointed cruise director. As a rule, these people were a godsend, stepping in to perform the task of establishing basic social conventions when nobody else would, or in this case, wanted to.

"I'm Polly Powhatten. Please call me Polly. I have a lab down the hall here, and, goodness, I guess I've been here ten . . . eleven years. I'm a pharmacologist. UCLA, Stanford. My doctorate is in biology, of course. The organisms we've been exposed to were meant to come to me, I'm afraid."

"Yeah, I'm still here," Dwayne stated, his ear to the phone. "I'm meeting Polly. She's the one who ordered the bugs."

She smiled. "I did. I'm researching the effects of freshwater plankton, gathered from inland ponds and lakes, on specific strains of bacteria. You see, the ecosystem of a standing body of water is similar to that of dark, moist land formations from which we get moss, mold, fungus . . . well, I can get into that some other time—if anyone cares to discuss it further, I should say. Yes, yes, some other day. I've been told I can go on and on when I'm excited about a new project, so be careful." She laughed. "And now you, Joanne. I think you told me the other day you were a student at Arizona State. Are you planning a career in biochemistry?"

"No," Joanne said, her voice very soft, barely audible. Studying the fingers in her lap, she went on, "I want to teach. Kindergarten. I'd"—she looked up at Polly—"I'd like to have a preschool someday. I like children. I like to listen to them laugh. I . . . well, I'm working here because I need the money. Dr. Andropov saw my card on campus, on the bulletin board, you know? Where you say you can do this or that and need a part-time job?"

"No, she finished, I guess," Dwayne told his girlfriend over the phone. "Now, ah, Joanne is saying she's from the college and she wants to teach little kids. I don't know, Joanne *who*—"

"It's Kriser," Joanne told him. "My name is Joanne Kriser. I guess I should have said that first."

"I hired Joanne because she was uniquely qualified for the job I needed her to do here," Kurt said, smiling kindly at the girl, who looked flustered and ill at ease. She returned his smile with gratitude and directed her gaze to her lap once again. "She's indispensable to me."

Joanne laughed softly and shook her head. "That's not really true," she said, looking up. "My card said 'need work, willing to learn.' Dr. Andropov said that if I could learn to reject phone calls, the job was mine. I type letters, too, sometimes, but mostly I just answer his phone for him and take messages."

"And what do I do with all those pretty pink notes you give me?"

She grinned at him. "Tear them up."

He didn't have to look at Dr. McKissack to know he'd made another direct hit. The room temperature shot up several degrees, and he could almost feel her sending daggers his way with her eyes.

He turned instead to speak to Dwayne. "Tell your lady friend that my name is Dr. Kurtsevo Andropov, and she may call me Kurt, too, if she'd care to. I'm a classic Taurus with my moon rising in Cancer, I believe. It's been a while, but the last time I was forced to have a luminary prediction cast upon my horizon, I was supposed to have a quiet, productive life with few, if any, hardships. Tell her something's gone terribly wrong."

He'd intended to be mildly amusing; to keep pace with what was fast becoming a tragic absurdity. He was delighted that his words could goad another tongue-lashing from the good Dr. McKissack.

"You know, it's a good thing you don't have to pay taxes on what you think you're worth, Doctor," she said while Dwayne continued to relay the message. "You're not the only person here who's been inconvenienced by this mess. The chance of one or all of us dying aside, Dr. Pow—Polly here, has to postpone her new project. I'm sure Joanne is missing school." She looked at Dwayne and decided he was already missing too much to mention. "And I happen to have a life of my own as well. This isn't just a hardship for you, you know. The rest of us aren't here by choice."

"Which is the only reason I'm allowing you to stay, Doctor," he said, amusement dancing in his eyes.

Allowing her to stay?

"Oh, my goodness, me," Polly said. "We're not really going to be calling each other 'doctor,' are we? It can be terribly confusing unless you're looking directly at the doctor you're speaking to. Then the other doctor will have to keep looking up to see if he or she is being looked at and—"

"People call me Mack," she said with a shrug. "It's short for McKissack, something I picked up in college. I work at the Centers for Disease Control and Prevention in Atlanta."

"Oh, my, yes. I heard about that business with Andropov-B. I was sad as could be. I hope it's not the bacteria."

"It's not," Kurt assured her.

"I hope not too," Mack said, ignoring him. "The A-B1 bacteria can make life so much better for so many people. Discovering it to be a pathogen is the last thing I want to do."

"Well, of course it is," Polly said, walking over to lean on the counter while she talked. "Has Kurt told you that I knew his famous daddy?"

"No. Ah . . . Kurt hasn't told me much of anything yet."

"Such a wonderful man," Polly said wistfully.

"The father, right?" Mack asked. She slid a direct glance in Kurt's direction. He grinned back at her, amused.

"Yes, dear. And so handsome. His accent . . . Oh, my goodness, yes. You wouldn't guess, but his accent could melt the walls of a nuclear fission chamber."

Mack couldn't help it. Her gaze met Kurt's across the work counter. He arched a brow and shrugged, as if to say the capacity to melt nuclear fission chambers was an inherent trait in his family and not something he could control.

"I've heard he was a very modest man," Mack said, sending Kurt an it-wouldn't-kill-you-to-be look.

"Gracious, yes. And shy, too, but that only added to his charm. Of course, I was already married to my Drew by then, but I remember the feeling I got whenever he smiled at me. Goodness, that was years and years ago. I wasn't much older than you, young man. And what is your name?"

"I'm Dwayne," the courier said, then, after listening to the phone for a second he added, "and this is Myrna. She says hi, and I'm supposed to tell you that her brother, Larry, owns Bio-Transport. That's the bio-transport service I work for."

"It's a pleasure to meet you both," Polly said happily. "I feel better now that we're all acquainted and have a basic understanding of one another. I'm sure the next few days will be trying for all of us. So much fuss. We're all frightened and anxious, but if we stick together and support one another, why, I think we'll muddle through this just fine."

Having to tolerate a cruise director was one thing—having to tolerate a perky, optimistic cheer-leader-type cruise director with a strange proclivity to rhyme was something else entirely.

"The man in the bathroom said something about food and beds," Mack said, looking around at the limited space. "I suppose we should—"

"The ladies can camp out in my office. Dwayne and I'll sleep in the wild," Kurt said, cutting her off, tipping his head toward the greenhouse. "Everything else will take place in the outer office when they're finished out there. My lab is off-limits. Is that understood?"

"Off-limits? I can't believe you," Mack said, her head pounding with tension. "We could all be dead in a week, and you'd deprive us of this much extra space to walk around in? Or are you afraid one of us will use our last dying breath to contaminate your project?"

"You may do whatever you wish with your last dying breath, Doctor. My concern is to prove that the A-B1 bacteria isn't harmful, and to prove it as fast as I can before it gets a bad reputation. It has too much potential to warrant the cloud of suspicion you're creating around it. I can't risk all the extra hands and chatter in my lab while I'm working."

"But I could help you," she said. "If we work together, we can prove it's safe in half the time. Polly can help too. We could have an answer before the quarantine is lifted."

"No. I work my way, in my time, *and* I work alone. End of discussion."

"That wasn't a discussion. That was *you* telling *us* how things are going to be around here and . . ." Her voice was getting too high and too loud. "Okay. Fine. Work alone, but you have to give up half your lab space. The rest of us will go stir-crazy if we can't use the limited space available to us."

He studied her for a long moment. The next two weeks were going to be anything but dull with her there. She was too bright, too plucky, and too tenacious to be controlled with something as simple as bad manners and a superior attitude. What worked well with the general populace wasn't going to work with her.

"A compromise, then," he said, enjoying the way she tried to hide her expression of victory. "While I'm working, each person comes in for an hour or two at a time, to read or write or to partake in some other sedentary, non-verbal activity. Does that seem fair to you, Doctor?"

"What about the greenhouse, and when you're not working?"

"The greenhouse is part of my lab. However, when I'm not working, you are all free to wander about, as long as you don't touch anything. Is that reasonable?"

She nodded. It was as reasonable as she expected him to get—for now. Where a man is willing to give up a millimeter, he will eventually give up a centimeter. Mack planned to go for the whole nine meters.

Dwayne cleared his throat loudly. "Am . . . am I . . . does anyone else smoke?" He looked at each of them hopefully. "I guess smoking is out then, huh?"

"Absolutely," Kurt said. He didn't give a whistle about the human lungs in the room; it would be bad for his plants. The others said nothing, but their expressions agreed that yes, it was pretty much out of the question.

"Oh, man, is this going to be a long two weeks." He paused. "Well, Myrna wants me to quit. 'Course, I could be dead tomorrow anyway."

During the next few hours cots, blankets, pillows, extra scrub gowns, a few current magazines, basic toiletries, a small portable television, and a variety of fruit juices and soft drinks were brought in. Meals were to be brought in on trays and removed after each feeding. That's what they called it—a feeding. In the hallway outside, they were becoming even more like test specimens.

Through the ceiling tiles, the contamination crew broke into the air ducts, which were then attached to a vacuum for filtration purposes. A large plastic tent, also air-locked, was pitched directly outside the door to protect the emergency-service personnel moving in and out of the contaminated area. The contaminants were given a phone number for questions, complaints, and requests. Medical histories were compiled for each of them. They reviewed an alternative fire plan. They were told a therapist was available if the stress became unbearable.

And then, rather unexpectedly, they were on their own. It was only two in the afternoon. By three, they were all ready to leave and go home.

"All right then," Kurt said, looking about as they stood or sat around his reception room, his hands in the pockets of his lab jacket. "We all have a place to sleep. Everyone knows the rules. I guess we're all set." He waited for a rebuttal. "I have work to do, so if you'll excuse me . . ."

"Who goes first?" Dwayne asked. He'd taken the time to set up his own cot in the greenhouse and to stow away a toothbrush and was back on the phone with Myrna. "With you, I mean. Myrna says we should go in alphabetical order, but drawing straws is okay with me too."

"Where do you think you're going with me?"

"Well, into your lab, like you said we could before."

"Oh." Kurt rubbed his forehead. "Tell you what, you decide among yourselves and surprise me. Okay?"

He'd turned and had his hand on the door knob when Mack said, "Good luck, Doctor."

He glanced back at her to see if she was being sarcastic.

"Thank you, Doctor, but I don't need luck. A few simple facts will prove A-B1 to be pure and healthy."

She nodded. "Good luck anyway."

THREE

He waited.

Dr. McKissack—Mack—wouldn't be able to resist her allotted time in his lab, and he was prepared to thwart her every attempt to involve herself in his experiments. He waited and found his concentration shallow, his mind wandering into the next room, wondering when someone, particularly Mack, would join him.

But as it happened, no one came.

An occasional burst of laughter informed him that his "cell mates" had found something else to do with their time. He suspected a grand gabfest was in progress. It was so typically female of them to start bonding with one another right away. They'd be friends before long, and thick as thieves soon after that; conspiring against him, worming their way into his lab, taking control of his experiment. . . .

Over his dead body. Let them giggle and twitter out there among themselves. He didn't care. He had work to do. The soil samples taken from the affected areas in Africa, the Ukraine, and the Yucatán were producing bacteria unlike any he'd seen before. If they were genetically similar to the A-B1 bacteria, they might be a mutation of the original bacteria, and if that were true, what was causing the mutation? If there was no specific discernible cause for the mutation, if it was spontaneous . . . well, then the last eight years of his life had been wasted. He'd have failed.

Another outburst of laughter had his eyes roving in the direction of the door. Had Mack said something amusing? Bright people generally had a sharp wit, not that she'd wasted any of her charm in his company. Still, she had a smile that came easily. He remembered it clearly. And what was she telling the others that might interest him? Having a clear handle on her personality could be helpful in keeping her out of his hair.

What if she mentioned what she did when she wasn't working; her plans for the future?

Not that he cared. Caring would denote an interest in her as something other than a fly in his ointment. More laughter had him glaring at the door. That's all she was, a fly in his ointment, a pest. His wife, *ex*-wife, had taught him all he needed to know about intelligent, dedicated women.

He forced himself to stay in his lab, admitting that with all that had gone on that day, he was bound to be a bit distracted. Finally Joanne tapped softly on the door to tell him the dinner trays had arrived.

They had a choice of beef, ham, or turkey submarine sandwiches; coleslaw, potato salad, pie for dessert, and a beverage. On such short notice, it was a step above the cafeteria food they'd expected, and no one complained.

Not that anyone would have noticed if Kurt had had a complaint. They sat across the room talking amiably, ignoring him.

"My mother said she'd be glad to stop and pick up anything any of you need," Joanne was saying. "Stationery. Shampoo. Whatever you want. She's waiting for my dad to get home from work, and then they're both coming over here. Do you think I'll be allowed to see them?"

"We'll have to call Eugene and see what he has planned for visitors," Polly answered. Eugene, according to the conversation, was the voice on the other end of the hotline for requests, questions, and complaints, their link to the outside. Kurt found it mildly nauseating that the situation had escalated so quickly into a big happy family affair—except for him. "Maybe they'll let your parents gown up and come in for a visit. Wouldn't that be exquisite? Visitors would certainly break up the monotony. Not that it's been boring so far. I must say that I'm rather proud of the way we're all handling this."

"My mom wanted to come, but I told her no. No money, ya know?" Dwayne said absently, picking the turkey and tomato out of his sandwich, leaving the lettuce and onion. "And I know Myrna's a no-show. She says her imagination is too vivid. The thought of invisible bugs would make her nuts, man. She's already mentioned a couple of times that she's glad it's me here and not her. I have a lot less imagination."

"Nonsense," Polly said. "From what I observed earlier, I'd have to say that your fear of invisible bugs is just as active as Myrna's, or anyone else's, for that matter. Nowhere near tranquillity. I also must tell you that I think you're handling your confinement with a great deal of courage and a remarkable sense of responsibility."

"You think so?"

"I do," Joanne said softly. With nothing short of awe, she added, "I thought it was wonderful the way you started the fire alarm while the rest of us were just standing there." She hesitated. "If Myrna can't bring you what you need, my parents will."

"Thanks," he said, nodding. "Thanks a lot."

She smiled at him shyly. Kurt wanted to throw up.

"You're not saying much over there, Doctor," Mack said, turning everyone's attention on him, unaware of the fact that she wasn't saying much either. "Did you solve any great mysteries this afternoon?"

"I'm afraid not, Doctor," he said, wiping his mouth with a napkin. "The greatest mysteries usually have the simplest solutions, and in this case, there may be no mystery at all."

"That's right," Dwayne said. "You've got a whole different bug you're working with back there. Myrna said she wouldn't sleep in the same room with bugs she couldn't see, but I figure if you're going to sleep in the greenhouse with them, well, they probably won't hurt me either." A brief pause. "Right?"

"Actually," Joanne said, touching Dwayne's arm tentatively. "Bacteria aren't like real bugs. They can move around a little, so scientists used to think they were animals, but then they discovered that the cell walls of bacteria were firm, like plants. Now they call most tiny organisms 'protists.' Not animals, not plants, but with characteristics of both. Dr. Andropov told me."

"And there's good ones and bad ones and his are good. Right?"

"That's not altogether true, either, dear," Polly said. "Some potentially harmful organisms lie about without causing the slightest bit of trouble, while less harmful organisms can do a great deal of damage, given the opportunity. Most are extremely useful in their place, but taken out of their element and put somewhere else, say into a human body, they can be deadly."

"But those in the greenhouse are safe enough, right?" Dwayne asked.

Kurt could see Mack preparing to negate this assumption as well by telling him her reason for being there. But unless Dwayne planned to eat the plants in the greenhouse, her words would only complicate things further.

"Right," he said before she could speak, telling the young man all he'd wanted to know in the first place. "We'll both be perfectly safe sleeping in the greenhouse. I don't even have a meat-eating mantis in my collection."

"Nothing that says, 'Feed me, Seymour, feed me now'?" Dwayne asked, grinning at Kurt, as if delighted to finally connect with the great doctor—even if it was with something as simple as a line from the movie *Little Shop of Horrors.*

Kurt smiled back, though he had no idea who Seymour was. You see, contrary to the opinions of people not in the know, he was not oblivious to the feelings of others. He might consider them silly or tedious or greatly exaggerated, but he was not oblivious to them. And if the boy, Dwayne, felt it was important to be amusing for him, so be it. He would try to be amused.

"So, what kind of bu-bacteria is it back there? What does it do?" Dwayne asked, feeling he now had an inside track with Kurt.

"Very simply put, they help feed plants. They act as a natural fertilizer."

"My goodness me," Polly said, laughing. "That *is* putting it simply. Come now. Next to Gaines wheat and IR-8 rice, the A-B1 bacteria is quite likely the biggest agricultural breakthrough since the plow."

"That's because it was genetically engineered," Mack said, seeing that Dwayne was lost in the "simply put." "Created. By Dr. Andropov."

Dwayne looked properly impressed. "Stellar, man. You actually made your own bug—bacteria?"

"Sort of."

"Oh yes, it's quite, ah, stellar," Polly said, wiggling in her seat beside Mack. "A brilliant continuation to his father's work. Boris would have been very proud of Kurt."

Mack almost fell off her chair watching Kurt lower his eyes to the floor and blush beet red to the roots of his dark hair. All along she suspected he'd be able to blush better than she could—but was that humility she was seeing? She blinked twice to refocus her eyes, curbing the urge to rub them in disbelief.

"I hadn't realized your father was a biochemist, too, Doctor," Joanne said, smiling, as if that were the sweetest thing she'd ever heard of—father/son biochemists.

"Goodness gracious, no, dear," Polly said before he could say anything. "Kurt's father was a simple country physician. In a lowly position. Or at least that's what he tried to make everyone believe."

"But that's exactly what he was, Polly," Kurt said simply. "That and a Russian immigrant who felt blessed to be an American."

Polly looked shocked. "Why, I hadn't realized you had such a gift for understanding facts, Kurt. Not many country doctors travel all over the world or work with other great scientists to develop new strains of grain that will feed the earth's population."

"That's true," he said, smiling a bit. "But he wouldn't have been traveling if he didn't feel he owed something for his freedom." And then speaking to the group, rather than to Polly only, he said, "His parents sent him out of Russia when he was fourteen, to live with his mother's brother here in the United States. His parents died shortly after that. He became a naturalized citizen and never went back, but he always remembered what it was like. His parents were poor farmers and he said there was never enough to eat."

"That was just before the Revolution, then," Mack said, as if thinking aloud. "Before the Bolsheviks took over. But emigrating still must have been very difficult. Especially if they were so poor."

He nodded. "He believed that his parents sold everything they owned and that he was smuggled out of the country. But, of course, at the time he was simply doing what and going where he was told to."

"How awful," Joanne said. Dwayne nodded sympathetically. "And he never saw his parents again?"

"No," Kurt said, talking about his father as if it wasn't an intrusion on his own life, as if he were merely reciting facts, giving a history lesson. "But he was very fond of his uncle, who was a medical doctor someplace in Pennsylvania for many years. They had a practice together for a while in the country, and then my father decided it was time to pay his debt to society, so to speak. He joined some missionaries on their way to India and the Middle East and spent most of the rest of his life traveling, setting up, and recruiting staff for medical clinics all over the world."

"He deserved another Nobel Prize for that. And more," Polly said. "Unfortunately, it's not what he's best remembered for."

"No. Actually his hobby, botany, brought him fame and a Nobel Peace Prize." All the Nobel Prizes were prestigious, but there was something about the Peace Prize that all men coveted. Even Kurt. "What's that old saying? You can take the boy off the farm, but you can't take the farm out of the boy. That was the case with my father, I guess. Even after he retired, he loved growing things. I grew up in a little house in Portland, Oregon. There were plants and flowers everywhere." He chuckled. "My mother used to say that if I'd had an allergy to pollen, she didn't know what my father would have tossed out first, me or his flowers." They laughed. "I was always sort of glad he never had to make that choice."

"Goodness me, this from the boy adored by his father," Polly said, almost in a scolding manner. Kurt smiled and looked away, as if wanting to keep some cherished memory to himself. "Tell them about the Gaines wheat, dear."

"Why don't you, Polly. You know the story as well as I do."

"But I like listening to you talk," she said.

Mack did, too, though she'd have cut off her own tongue before she said so. His voice was deep and smooth and calming.

"Me too," Dwayne said. "I mean, this story is out there, man. Did he end up as a wheat farmer or what?"

"No," Kurt said, smiling, enjoying the attention his fellow inmates were now bestowing on him, as if he were one of them. "Everywhere he traveled in those days, he saw that the greatest cause of death was starvation, for which the only cure is, of course, food. I can't imagine anything more frustrating than knowing a simple solution to a problem and not being able to provide it. I'm sure it was hard for him," he said. "During the war—World War II—he volunteered for duty and was stationed at a hospital in the Philippines. Afterward he stayed on awhile to do what he could for the locals. They'd been very helpful in the war effort," he added. "He was in Manila when the Green Revolution began."

"The what? Green Revolution? Never heard of it," Dwayne said.

"Lots of people haven't," Kurt said. "It was an international movement to bring about peace by feeding the world."

"Oh. Cool. A hippie thing. Like make peace, not war."

"Gracious, dear, you are young," Polly said. "It was make love, not war. And that came *after* the Green Revolution."

"That's right," Kurt said. "The Green Revolution was nearly over by then. You're thinking of another revolution entirely."

"People thought the earth was a starving planet after the war," Mack said, having only read this information of late. "American farmers were about the only ones keeping it alive, and they could only manage that for about twenty years before their own land dried up and blew away too."

"A starving planet? You're kidding. The whole planet?"

"Oh my, yes. That's what they thought. What a mess. It was dreadful. The population of the world had outdistanced the capacity to feed itself. Too many people, not enough food." Polly leaned back in her chair and crossed her arms over her belly. "Everyone was terrified. Suddenly we had population control, and societies all over the world were decreasing the size of the average family. People were choosing to have no children at all rather than add to the problem."

"A stitch in time saved nine," Mack muttered thoughtfully. She was surprised that anyone heard.

"That's it exactly," Polly said. "The increase in birth control, along with the development and distribution of high-yielding grains and modern farming techniques, saved the world in the nick of time."

Dwayne looked fascinated.

"But I thought there was a baby *boom* after that war," Joanne said, puzzled.

"There was. Here in America. Everyone was so happy to have survived the war, they refused to believe they'd end up starving to death," Polly said. "And as it happened, they didn't."

"It was the high-yield grain that won Dr. Andropov's father the Nobel Prize," Mack said. "The United States already had Gaines wheat. It's a bit shorter with a thicker stalk and heavier heads of grain than regular wheat. It was Dr. Andropov's thought that if they could get rice and corn to do the same thing, they'd double the world's food production."

She looked over Dwayne's shoulder to find Kurt watching her with interest, his too-blue eyes fixed and intense. Her mouth went dry.

"I'm sorry. Go on with the story, Doctor," she said, feeling like a sixth grader caught talking in class. She was beginning to dislike, fervently, the way he kept looking at her. It was as if she were a specimen of the female gender he hadn't encountered before. He was acting like a bird-watcher observing a triple-breasted bimbo tootsie in the wild.

"You were doing fine, Doctor, and there isn't much left to tell," he said. "At the Rice Research Institute in the Philippines, he added his botanical knowledge to that of some of the world's greatest scientists, and they came up with IR-8. They called it the miracle rice."

"They solved the starvation problem? So how come they still have those commercials with the starving babies on TV? Man, Myrna just hates those commercials."

"We all hate those commercials, dear, but the fact remains that there are still people starving on this planet," Polly said. "IR-8 was only the first step in solving the hunger problem. After that, it had to be distributed worldwide; they had to teach people how to grow it; they needed to export millions of tons of fertilizers to feed it. And, of course, the good men like Boris, who developed the grains, had nothing to do with its distribution. Governments and big business, like Agro-Chem here, took over. It simply follows that where there is a great deal of good, there is also some bad. Very sad. Some people are still starving."

Dwayne frowned and leaned back thoughtfully in his chair, as if taking a moment to let it all soak in. A momentary lull settled over the conversation. Mack was about to use it as an opportunity to excuse herself, to find a place to hide herself away from the small talk and social amenities—and from Kurt's eyes. But then Dwayne spoke again.

"So, Doc, what are your bugs for? I thought most farmers hated bugs."

Kurt laughed. It was an unexpected sound that she found . . . nice. Throaty and mellow. Natural. Engaging. Maybe she wouldn't leave just yet. Maybe he'd laugh again.

"That is another very long, very boring story, my friend," he told Dwayne.

"And I suppose you have a bus to catch," Polly said.

"Tell them what you're working on. Go on." She leaned forward to the two young people. "This is fascinating."

"Polly," he said, looking extremely reluctant. "I've had people tell me that it's as boring as wet cardboard. Maybe tomorrow . . ."

Polly pointed a knobby index finger at him. "I know who that was, and I won't listen to a word of it. Not a bit. How can a man's lifework be boring? You don't believe that nonsense, do you?"

"Of course not, but I'm afraid that to people who aren't interested in it themselves, it can be tiresome."

That was Mack's experience as well. As a whole, most people didn't care about disease-causing microbes unless they themselves were at risk, or unless they, too, were epidemiologists. She'd found this to be true of most specialized professions. Physicians preferring the company of other physicians; writers preferring other writers; lawyers didn't get along with anyone, generally; but biochemists preferred other biochemists; housewives preferred other housewives; students other students. . . . Her opinion of him was mildly swayed by his sensitivity to this phenomenon.

With encouragement from the unsuspecting Dwayne and Joanne, Kurt started to explain the nitrogen cycle—God's recipe for keeping soil rich with nutrients.

Mack slipped away, as the lecture on the dangers of man-made fertilizers began. She knew the material. She could ace a test on the A-B1 bacteria, a microbe genetically engineered not only to produce its own ammonia supply but to "fix" nitrogen for its host plant, specifically IR-8 rice, as well.

It was a wondrous project she'd followed since she was a freshman in college and the rumors of an ex-Texas A&M football player/graduate student, the son of a

Nobel laureate, won a Kingsford Grant to study his theories for a perpetual, self-renewing, onetime fertilizer that would redefine farming practices all over the world.

If anyone had a right to be conceited and pompous, she grudgingly admitted that Kurt probably did. Using the light of a glowing desk lamp to pick her way through the lab, she indulged in a moment of truth. What she really resented was that he was living her dream . . . he was making a difference.

There was nowhere else to go but into the greenhouse—it was as far from the others as she could get. Was it strange that she spent half her time avoiding people and the other half feeling lonely and alone? Her mother would certainly think so, and truth be told, Mack suspected she might be right.

She couldn't remember if she'd always preferred her own company, but she was increasingly aware of this inclination over the past few years. She had friends, *good* friends and many acquaintances, everywhere she'd traveled. But there was always something missing—not in them but in her.

She bent forward to smell a stunning red blossom, hoping the scent would help her identify the flower. The pungent odor wasn't one she recognized, but it triggered something in her mind. A memory of a dream she had, which recurred now and again. It was a vivid dream that would wake her from her sleep, seemingly more real than actual events in her life.

She shivered as a chill raced up her spine and along her arms. Quickly, she looked about for something else to occupy her mind.

The greenhouse smelled wonderful. Sweet. Earthy. A little like the Yazoo early in the summertime, when the magnolias, trillium, and violets mixed their scents with the muddy waters and the deep, rich soil of the Delta.

"You gonna sit on the porch all summer," she could hear her daddy saying, his voice as thick and slow as the Delta waters he loved. "Or are ya gonna take off those pretty little shoes and come play in the mud with me?"

She inhaled deeply, trying to recall more of the long lazy summers she'd spent with him, knee-deep in warm mud, catfish farming, or spread-eagle in a sweet-potato field with the sun on her face and bees buzzing in her ears.

He was a huge man, taller than the trees, with humor-filled eyes that made you feel like a princess and a smile you'd do anything, *anything* to see.

"You are like a brand-new penny, shinin' in the sunshine. The prettiest thing I ever did see. Bright. Excitin'. I wanna pick you up and put ya in my pocket. Keep you there forever."

She sighed and felt wistful.

The sun was setting in the west somewhere, what light that was left filtered through the skylight and the outer wall of the greenhouse. There was nothing to see but green plants, the foliage so dense and lush, she was only presuming the wall on the other side was made entirely of glass.

She found the two cots the men had set up well away from the planting troughs, which had been moved to one side for safety.

Hesitating briefly, wondering which cot belonged to Kurt and which was Dwayne's, she sat on the closest one, deciding she really didn't care. She'd smooth out the wrinkles when she got up, and no one would ever know she'd been there.

She was good at that, smoothing wrinkles, making

her presence invisible to those who came behind her. Walking softly. Speaking calmly. Leaving no footprints. Leaving the wind undisturbed as it whistled through the leaves. A true lady never caused a ripple in society's pond, her mother used to say. If she wanted to see herself in it, she kept it as clear and smooth as a looking glass.

She closed her eyes and let her brain drain, a secret she'd learned as a child. If you couldn't think, you couldn't feel. And if you couldn't feel, nothing hurt. It was a good trick, but it never lasted long.

Andropov-B. A safe subject for her weary mind to feed on, yet it skipped directly to it's creator, Andropov, K.

Andropov, K.? Her eyes popped open and she sat up straight as her spine went rigid with realization. If he'd named the bacteria after himself, as she had accused him of earlier, why wasn't it A-K1? It was A-B1 because he'd named it after his father, Boris.

"Hiding?"

"What?" She all but jumped out of her skin.

"I'm sorry. I guess . . ." Kurt stopped speaking, to watch as she sprang from the cot, smoothed the bedding, fluffed the pillow that hadn't been touched, then turned to face him—at attention, with her hands behind her back. ". . . you were hiding."

"From what?" she asked, off guard and defensive.

"How should I know? You're the one sitting in here in the dark alone."

"Well, I wasn't hiding. Why would I hide? I was . . . collecting my thoughts. Thinking."

He raised his brows and nodded, letting the door to the lab swing closed. "This is a good place to think. Carry on."

How was it that he could step into a room and make

it seem smaller? Make the muscles in her shoulders ache with tension? Make her heart lurch and twist; beat faster and faster as he walked toward her? Well, she actually knew how it was, and she wished it would stop.

"Thanks," she said, her hands falling forward to her sides. She shrugged. "I'm not in the mood anymore." She stepped away from the cots. "I think I'll just say good night to the others and—"

"Find someplace else to hide?" he said, cutting off her polite excuse to leave him.

He was standing just to the left of her. She looked to the right. "Doctor, if you're trying to make me angry . . ."

"I won't succeed, will I?" he said more than asked. He wasn't sure why he was goading her. Maybe because he was tired. Maybe because it was so easy for her to walk away from him; to ignore him when all he wanted was to crack her open like a walnut, just to see what was inside. Or maybe . . . he could sense an unhappiness about her, because it was so much like his own.

"It was my impression that you succeed at everything you strive for, Doctor. However, if making me angry is now a goal, and if all your goals are so pointless and petty, your success rate no longer surprises me."

"Aha! That's it," he said, suddenly animated, his fingers straight up, thumbs together for a cameraman's view. "A little more feeling. Some attitude. Squint your eyes a little, and that might have hurt."

"I haven't the slightest desire to hurt you, Doctor." Kill him maybe, but that didn't necessarily have to hurt. "But if it'll make you feel any better, you're no Steven Spielberg. I doubt you could direct your way out of a paper bag," she said, her performance serene. "So don't give up your day job."

He nodded, pleased. "Just in case no one has told you before, that other business doesn't really work."

Her expression was torpid. "What doesn't work?" she asked, sounding bored.

"The Southern-belle routine," he said, smiling. He leaned closer as if to tell her a secret. "When you're angry your eyes light up like emeralds. Your voice gets husky with passion, and that drawl you want so badly to forget gets as thick as honey." He moved his head slightly to look directly into her eyes. "It's the sexiest thing I ever heard."

She wasn't breathing. Damn. And her mind was empty—except for a particular awareness of the size and closeness of his body, the shape of his lips, the unfathomable depths of his eyes, the soapy-musk scent she enjoyed so much—but completely empty of anything resembling wit or control. Worst of all, she was the first to look away.

He chuckled. "Come on, Mack, you can do it," he said, his voice soft and encouraging. "You made the choice to limit yourself to one weapon; now use it. Tear me apart with your choice selection of ladylike words. Make me bleed."

Her fingers curled into fists at her sides. She remembered blood trickling from Galen Osgood's nose after he splashed mud on her best white tights and her Sunday shoes with his bike . . . and the longest, hottest afternoon she ever spent in her bedroom, waiting for her mother's punishment.

"Don't be ridiculous, Doctor. Why would I want to make you bleed?"

He frowned. "That's it? You just give in? Just like that?"

She cast him a derisive look. "She who walks away lives to fight another day. Good night, Doctor."

He watched her leave, a slow smile forming on his lips. She was no quitter. He knew as well as he knew his own name, she'd be back the next day with a battle plan and a full array of weapons to use against him. And it didn't matter if their contest was on a personal or a professional level, she'd never let him win. She'd back off, regroup, and attack again and again before she'd ever surrender.

Now his interest in her was more than merely piqued. His objective was no longer simply to crack her open for a look-see. He would settle for nothing less than surrender. He would know her secrets and her dreams. She would place herself in the palm of his hand, and he would crush her spirit—and that damnable stubborn streak of hers . . .

Or not.

FOUR

It was always a party. The people in the dream kept referring to it as a "Celebration of Life," but it looked more like a New Year's Eve party. There was a lot of joyous hugging and kissing, laughter and warm smiles. Friends from the past and the present were there, from all over the world, and everyone knew one another. No one was a stranger. No one felt left out . . . except Mack.

They were all so pleased to see her. She was nervous. It had taken her a long time to get ready and she was late arriving at the party. She accepted a hundred compliments on her looks with humble gratitude; even her mother said she'd never looked more lovely. She walked through the crowd with her arms at her sides, realizing that the party was in her honor. They were all there because they loved her, they liked her, they were her friends.

The kisses were a bit awkward. They'd press their heart-warmed lips to her cheek, and she would purse her lips and smack at the air close to their ears, feeling insincere and robotic. The hugs were the worst of it. She would lean into their arms, eager to be held, and they'd hold her close for several seconds before pulling away with hurt expressions on their faces. She hadn't hugged them back. She wanted to, but her arms were like lead weights at her side, her elbows rusted in an extended position.

Some of her friends and loved ones would try over and over to embrace her, and she would try harder and harder to hug them back, until finally they walked away, hurt and dejected.

"It's not you," she'd call after them. "It's me. I want to hug you. Please, let's try it one more time."

Someone else would try, but to no avail.

"Don't give up on me," she'd call out, her heart aching to feel their arms about her once again. "I want you to hold me."

People she barely knew, but admired and wanted to know better, would stand with their arms about her shoulders, or stroke her with affection. They'd caress her cheek with their hands, looking hopeful, the desire to be close to her clear in their faces.

"Go ahead, hug me," she'd say. "I want you to. I can't hold you in my arms, but that doesn't mean I don't care about you. I want to hug you, too, but . . . my arms are broken, I think. I can't move them. Can't you pretend I'm hugging you back?"

The disappointment on their faces would bring tears to her eyes.

"Please. I need you to hold me. I want you to touch me. Please," she'd say, running after them, her arms all but dragging on the floor, useless. She'd press her body against the next person she saw, cuddle close, trying with all her might to show how much she loved them. But without her arms to hold them, they'd stare at her in confusion, back away as if she were demented.

"Please, please. Somebody hold me," she'd say, crying. "I need to be held."

Hands belonging to the friendly faces around her would reach out to her. Touch her arms and back. Smooth out her hair, massage her neck, gently pat her cheek. Only a few hands, those of old lovers, would fondle her breasts, trail heat down the center of her abdomen, tickle her inner thighs. She'd feel herself quicken. She'd writhe with desire as more hands reached out to her, poking and pinching. One slapped her, and she cried out, "No! Stop! Don't touch me."

But the hands continued. Soothing, exciting, hurting all at once. Suddenly her own hands rose up before her eyes. Coming closer and closer; getting bigger and bigger until they covered her face entirely. She sobbed into them, knowing that if only she'd been able to reach out and hold the people she loved, they wouldn't have hurt her.

But rather than a comfort, or a cover for her shame and sorrow, her hands pressed close to her face, tighter and tighter. At first she didn't understand it, then she understood too well. They were going to kill her. She rolled her head back and forth but couldn't dislodge them. They pressed harder. She couldn't breathe through her nose. She opened her mouth, gasping for air. She couldn't get any. She tried to scream. No sound. Suffocating, her heart pounding louder and louder, faster and faster, more and more violently. She was about to die. . . .

She awoke, sitting straight up in bed, sobbing and gasping. Only one hand remained, and it was placed lightly across her forehead. She grabbed at it, catching it hard about the wrist.

A pained gasp. "I'm sorry, Doctor. I . . . I heard you moaning. I . . . I thought you might be ill."

Breathing hard, but breathing, it was several seconds before she recognized Joanne's gentle voice; before she could focus on the dark shadows of the two cots across the room. Something, hopefully Polly, was making noises like an elephant breaking wind. She slackened her grip as she pushed Joanne's hand away from her.

"I'm . . . it was a dream, is all. I'm sorry I woke you."

"That's okay. Are you all right?"

"I'm fine," she said shortly, embarrassed. "I'm . . . sorry. Please, go back to sleep if you can."

"Okay." Joanne hesitated. "Can I get you some water or something?"

"No. Thank you." But the water was a good idea. She knew *she* wouldn't be going back to sleep. "In fact, I think I'll get up and get some myself. Please, go back to bed."

It was too dark to see the girl's expression, but she saw the nod of her head and could sense her concern. It was sweet and annoying at once.

"Good night, Doctor."

"Good night, Joanne." Her voice sounded harsh and angry in her ears, and Joanne deserved neither. "Joanne?" she called out in a whisper. "Please call me Mack."

There was a moment of silence before Joanne's soft, friendly and gratified voice murmured, "Good night, Mack."

She slipped quietly out of the office into the waiting room, closing the door without a sound. She took in her first good deep breath and blew it out quickly, satisfied that she would have no more trouble breathing.

She was glad to be awake, but the prospect of another sleepless night brought tears of frustration to her eyes. For months now, if she slept at all, her repose was light and fitful or deeply disturbed by the dreams. Most nights, however, she would prowl whatever hotel room she was staying in until four or five in the morning, fall into a deep dreamless sleep at dawn, and awake groggy and exhausted a couple of hours later, in time to go to work.

There was a window to the outside in the waiting room, but it cast only enough light to differentiate the blackness of night from the blackness of solid objects. She could see a few stars in the sky and, in the distance, the tiny lights of Phoenix . . . or maybe Scottsdale or Mesa. She wasn't even sure which direction she was facing.

Earlier they'd moved all the furniture but the desk out of the office and into the waiting room. There was a tall-backed leather chair to her left a few feet, if she recalled correctly, groping in the dark with her hands.

"Six more inches," came a voice from the shadows.

A tiny yelp of fear escaped her, her knees buckled with terror, and she staggered the last few inches to the chair, falling into it, gasping for air once again.

Curse him. He should wear a bell.

"Jumpy, aren't you?"

"Not . . . not as a rule, no. But don't let that spoil all your fun, Doctor." She couldn't distinguish his form from the shadows, but his voice was coming from the leather couch under the window. She assumed he was lying on it. "What are you doing out here, rehearsing for Halloween?"

"Don't you think that if I'd known I was going to be treated with a visit from you, I might have been a little . . . trickier?"

"Absolutely."

"Good. I wouldn't want you to be underestimating me."

There was a brief opportunity to inform him that she didn't need to underestimate him because he clearly *over-* estimated himself, but she let it go. She wasn't in a stinging mood.

"Never."

"Then I'll tell you why I'm out here, Doctor. I haven't fit on a cot since I was twelve years old, and I've spent many a comfortable night on this couch. So, I'm sleeping here."

And she'd disturbed his sleep too.

"I'm sorry," she said. "I'm waking everyone up tonight, it seems. I hope you'll be able to fall back to sleep. I'm truly sorry I disturbed you."

She stood and was about to leave, to lie awake in her bed all night, when he spoke.

"I wasn't asleep. Stay if you like." His glib tone surprised him. Imagine, thinking of her, and suddenly she's there. He'd thought he was dreaming at first.

"Thank you, but I think I'll go back and try again. I—"

"Stay. Please." He was again startled by how much he wanted her there, across the room from him, in the dark, her soft voice like a beacon in a storm. "Maybe we can work on that, ah, truce you were talking about earlier."

Blankets rustled, and she could see he was sitting up now.

"You want to talk about Andropov-B now? In the middle of the night?"

"No," he said, very definite. "But I'm willing to discuss most anything else, if you feel like talking."

"Oh." He was by no means cooperating. He was simply trying to be nice. "Well, no, I don't really feel like—"

"Tell me about Mississippi. I've never been there."

She smiled. "This is very kind of you, Doctor, and . . . very unexpected, but it's not necessary. I got up for a drink of water, that's all."

"Fine. Get me one too."

Not many modern American males would make a statement like that without adding please and/or a long explanation as to why they couldn't get up and get their own water. Obviously, his ego problem was more serious than she thought.

Wordlessly, she took a few steps to the small refrigerator that was brought in to keep their drinks and fruit snacks cool, and removed a bottle of water. She filled a *single* glass, put the water away, and returned to the high-backed chair.

He chuckled. "Most Southern women would have graciously overlooked that minor breach of etiquette, or at least gotten me the water and then pointed it out to me. You must be of mixed blood. Let me guess, Southern and California radical, or . . . Southern and Northeast blunt. Maybe, it's Southern and Midwestern straightforward I'm detecting?"

"Maybe it's just Southern and sick of it," she said helpfully, mildly amused by his descriptions. He laughed softly, and her heart lurched. She *did* like that sound.

"I confess, that one hadn't occurred to me." He stood to get his own glass of water. He liked talking to her. He was never sure what she'd say next.

She could tell by the well-defined lines of his silhouette that his shirt was missing. Squinting in the dark, she was only half-relieved to see less definition below his waist.

"Tell me," he said, redirecting her attention in a hurry. "Did you have to take assertiveness classes, or does your candor and blunt delivery come naturally to you?"

She smiled.

"I call it a delayed and prolonged adolescent rebellion." Again he chuckled, and she found herself wanting to make him do it once more; found herself wanting to be friends. She did. Amazing. Or . . . perhaps it was as simple as needing to talk, and the darkness and a stranger making it easy. Either way, she went on. "Actually, it's my mother who's the aristocratic guardian of gracious Southern living—made legendary by nineteenth-century robber barons and slave owners, no less."

"I see. And your father?"

She smiled and shook her head fondly, but it was the tender elation in her voice that hinted at her sentiments. "My daddy was the devil in disguise. A big handsome charming man with a gift for words and romance . . . and too much confidence for poor white trash. He grew up catfish farming on the Yazoo . . . swept my mother clean off her feet on a romp through Vicksburg one summer. She never forgave him for it."

He was leaning against the small refrigerator, his long legs stretched out in front of him—crossed perhaps, as she could see only one bare foot in the silver light from the window. He seemed to be studying her, though she knew he couldn't see her any better than she could see him.

"Or let you forget it, correct?" he said, as if he'd read her story in a book somewhere.

"I believe she tried to . . . overlook it, most of the time. The family fortune was old enough and large enough that her sin was eventually forgiven. But like you say, not forgotten. Poor thing, she was left with the burden of providing proof that her progeny was worthy of the family name. Lucky for me, she was convinced that my weaker genes weren't something I couldn't overcome. If I tried hard enough."

"What about your father? What sort of relationship did you have with him?"

"A good one. He would have married my mother, but she wouldn't have him. I, on the other hand, was glad to have him. He swept me off my feet, too, regularly. Every summer, for six whole weeks, he'd carry me off to his catfish farm. He died in a hunting accident when I was sixteen."

"I'm sorry."

His bare chest, the sincerity in his hushed voice, his bare feet in the silvery light, the darkness, the quiet of the night, the stars outside the window—all made for an intense uneasiness on her part. He didn't seem to notice the intimacy in the air. He wasn't breathing a little too fast. He wasn't keeping both hands clasped firmly about an empty glass to keep from rubbing goose bumps off his skin.

"Me too," she said abruptly, suddenly aware that she'd lapsed into silence. "I mean, about your father . . . about what I said this morning."

He laughed. "You said a great many things this morning."

"I'd forgotten your father's name was Boris. I didn't

know you'd named the bacteria after him and not yourself."

"Ah. So am I now less conceited in your opinion?" he asked in a light and teasing tone, half imagining he could smell sunshine.

"No," she said in a like tone.

She saw his head nod and a faint gleam of teeth when he smiled.

"A beautiful, ambitious, *truthful* woman who can admit she's been wrong. You're a rare find, Doctor." What could she say? "We're something alike, I think. In some ways."

"Such as?"

"Such as being flawed products of our environments." He waited for her to say something, and when she didn't he continued. "My own father had the opposite effect on my life. I barely remember him. He married my mother late in his life; he was an old man when I was born. I have a few scattered memories, but primarily he's this bigger-than-life storybook hero who hung a ridiculous Russian name on me and died before he could take me to my first baseball game."

"And you resent him for that?"

"No. I resent people who expect me to mimic him."

"Your mother?"

There was a long silence as he walked back across the room and settled himself on the couch again. He hadn't been imagining that scent of sunshine; it was her scent, filling the air around him, spreading through his mind like wild Virginia creeper, turning his thoughts to flowers and lace. . . . He was better off on this side of the room.

"My mother adored him," he said, missing the smell of sunshine in a way he never had before. "She was one of his young students when they met—one of those Polly talks about—who followed him everywhere and hung on his every word. This was the late fifties, when bomb shelters were big and only the super-intellectuals were preaching peace and harmony and world ecology. . . . And of course, women like Polly Powhatten and my mother—career women, they call them now, I suppose—were few and far between. Women who would put up with the traveling he did, who understood what he was talking about, who'd tolerate his plants and experiments, for a greater cause."

"Did you become a brilliant biochemist to please her?"

"No," he said, and laughed. "She wasn't like that. There was a certain standard of excellence that had to be maintained, naturally, but she attributed my brilliance to the joining of her genes with his. She felt studying was an obligation I owed myself, more than anyone else."

"Good for her," she said, far more interested in his mother now than his father. "So you could have been anything you wanted to be."

"Pretty much, yes." He went silent for a moment. "She used to try and help me hide who I was. I know how that sounds, but it's hard being the son of a Nobel laureate. And if you're reasonably bright, other people's expectations become a heavy burden. Especially when you're young and you don't understand. Later it just makes you angry."

She nodded. She knew this sort of resentment.

"So, who were these other people?"

"Teachers mostly, guidance counselors. After my father died, my mother went back to school to get her doctorate. She taught for a long time at Lewis and Clark College; spent her summers researching marine life, chasing whales and dolphins, tracking the migration pattern of seals and penguins. . . ."

"And wasn't around much?"

"Not in the summertime, and she was busy during the school year. But she did understand what was happening to me, when I could finally talk about it." He sighed. "It felt as if they had a whole different grading system for me. I was above-average smart, but they were expecting a prodigy, as if my father were a genius and the gift was hereditary. They pushed, and nothing I did was exceptional enough. I wasn't working hard enough or I could do better if I wanted to. The pressure to please them got so great that I missed half of third grade with stomach ulcers. That's when my mother stepped in. She put me in another school, made sure none of the records had information about my father. But, sure enough, someone found out, and it started all over again."

"Didn't she talk to the teachers? Couldn't she make them stop?"

"She tried. She moved me to two more schools before she finally decided Portland was too small a place in which to keep a secret. She sent me to live with my uncle in Spokane, and my heritage followed me there too. I felt branded. I couldn't make anyone understand that I wasn't my father. And even if I were, he was never as intelligent as they expected me to be."

"What did you finally do?"

He shook his head. "Same as you, I suspect. Nothing. Clenched my teeth and put up with it. Did the best I could to keep them happy. Rebelled in a secret, quiet fashion most of the time, and then I'd occasionally shock them all by doing something outrageous."

She'd never told a soul about the overdose of chocolate Ex-Lax she'd taken the night before the Spring Co-tillion, the annual ball at which she and ten other young ladies of good blood and great wealth were to be presented to Vicksburg society. She was so weak and exhausted from the diarrhea, even her mother had seen the wisdom of sending those last-minute regrets—though she bemoaned the blow that mysterious illness had had on Mack's social life for years afterward.

"All through high school I wore nothing but black. Everything I owned was black," she said, confiding in him. "It didn't matter to me what color I wore, I just picked black and stuck to it. It nearly drove my mother to drink."

"What else?"

"A few times, long before the cancer scare, I got sunburned on purpose, before a garden party or some barbecue she was desperate for me to attend, generally at the home of some young man she pictured as a future son-in-law. I was so ugly, she'd make me stay home. She'd go, and make up some elaborate fib on my behalf."

"What a dreadful child you were."

"What did you do?"

"I played football—a dangerous sport and total waste of time for someone with my talents, as you well know," he said, being facetious. "And I'd flunk one subject a semester. Straight A's in all but one class, then the next term I'd excel in that and fail something else. They knew it was a game, and it irritated the hell out of them."

She laughed.

"That's nice," he said.

"What?"

"Hearing you laugh. You should do it more often."

Hadn't she just wished to hear him laugh more too?

She cleared her throat uncomfortably. "It's getting late. We should try to get some sleep, I guess."

"Was it as painful as that?"

"What?"

"Talking to me? You hardly told me anything, and yet you're running off to hide again."

"Hardly. I'm tired."

"Probably. But you won't sleep."

She sighed loudly. "There are none so ignorant as those who know it all." Except this time he was right. "My mother has a quote or an adage or a proverb for everything. She can be very annoying."

"And you haven't called her to tell her what's happened, have you?" It was a statement more than a guess.

"You can be very annoying too."

"You'll get used to it. It takes a while, but eventually everyone warms up rather nicely to me. You will too."

"Not even if we were cremated together."

He laughed, then sobered. "When are you going to call her?"

"When I have something to tell her. She's used to me being gone for long periods of time. I can't see the sense in worrying her about this quarantine, unless I'm infected. She frets enough as it is."

"What about your office? Won't they be in contact with her? To keep her informed?"

"I haven't called them either."

"Why not?"

"They can't do anything to get me out of this. I don't have anything to report on A-B1." She shrugged. "I'll call them when I do have something to report."

She hadn't called anyone, he realized. Even he'd called his mother in Portland and his neighbor, asking him to keep an eye on his house. He'd canceled a date for

Saturday night. Was there no one in her life who'd be missing her in two weeks?

"You said *when* you have something to report," he said, thinking it best to steer the conversation in a different direction. "Were you speaking of being infected or of Andropov-B?"

"Yes."

He took in a deep breath through his nose and rolled back onto the couch, stretching out, crossing his arms over his chest.

"You're one of those extremely stubborn women, aren't you, Doctor?"

"I can be."

"I can be stubborn as well."

"I'm sure."

"I thought we should be cordial, confined here as we are, but our talking in the dark like this isn't going to change things in my lab. I work alone."

"So you've said."

"And so I meant."

"Fine."

"I want to be sure we understand one another."

"I think we understand one another perfectly, Doctor."

And they did. By providence, profession, and preference they were attracted to each other, and the force field between them was a maze of veiled walls, vacuums, and worm holes. Each was a challenge to the other. Each was determined to cross the force field alive. Each was looking forward to running the gauntlet.

"Have you had much medical training?" he asked casually.

"Some. Will I be needing it? Are you planning to get physical with me?"

She'd meant to be amusing, but the long awkward silence that followed was thick with innuendo and double entendre.

"Perhaps," he said finally. "But I was actually thinking of monitoring ourselves and the others for signs of infection. Any symptom at all and . . ." The thought of total isolation was far worse than anything they could imagine in the next two weeks together.

"I know." She waited. "What are you thinking?"

"The emergency-service team will check us twice a day, but a lot can happen in twelve hours. You and I should keep an eye on the others, and each other. Being subtle, you understand, without alarming them. Check manually for fever, watch for rashes, that sort of thing."

"All right." She stood to leave. They weren't going to discuss their personal lives any further; that would be too personal. They weren't going to talk shop; that would never happen—according to Kurt. They weren't going to spar with words; that would be too dangerous to the delicate balance between them. There was nothing left to say or do but leave. "I'll see you in the morning then. Good night."

"Mack?"

"Yes?" She let her hand fall away from the doorknob.

After several seconds he said, "If . . . if anything should happen . . . to me, I mean . . ."

"Doctor? Are you trying to tell me that I can have your lab, and the bacteria, over your dead body?" she asked, interrupting a question that could have been difficult for both of them.

A soft laugh. "I'm trying to tell you that I'd appreciate it if you'd finish my tests for me, if I should become ill. I'm asking you to prove yourself wrong."

From behind the moon, around the stars, over the mountains, under the ocean, across the Great Plains, and through the hedge backward, she *thought* he was paying her a compliment.

"It would be an honor, sir."

FIVE

She walked into the lab and slammed the door.

Kurt looked up scowling.

"I'm first," she announced.

"And how did you manage that? Arm wrestling?" he asked.

"Actually, I drew the short straw," she said, making it sound more as if she were the loser than the winner of the first two-hour mini-vacation in the lab. She gave him a simpering smile.

It was only nine-thirty, and already the five of them had fallen into a routine. They were out of bed between six and seven, depending on one's habits and ability to sleep through the morning noise of the others. They took turns in the shower. Then they waited in the outer office to give blood samples and have their vital signs taken before the breakfast trays arrived.

By nine, it was as if the most exciting part of the day was over.

By popular consensus, no one spoke of the dark threat looming before all of them. They could have been five people caught in the Twilight Zone together—five people who knew it was only a thirty-minute episode and were determined to get through it as if nothing were unusual.

Kurt shut himself up in his lab. Polly disappeared behind the morning newspaper, the reference books she'd requested stacked in readiness on the table beside her. Joanne's parents had made arrangements for her to keep up with her studies. Her schoolbooks, notebooks, and paper were delivered in a large trunklike suitcase that also contained jeans and T-shirts, nighties, clean underwear, a stuffed animal, several romance novels, a needlepoint kit, a Walkman and tapes, and two three-dimensional puzzles. She'd given one of the puzzles to Dwayne, who, after talking with Myrna until it was time for her to go to work at the health-food store, set right to work putting the Empire State Building together.

"I wish I had a cigarette, man. If I had a cigarette, this would be easier. I think better when I'm smokin', you know." No one doubted it for a second.

Mack took to pacing the room, her job on hold, her hobbies nonexistent, her interest in television even worse. She tried to start up a conversation, but her three companions were rather . . . preoccupied. She flipped through the last *YM* magazine she hadn't as yet flipped through and gave a disparaging look to the copy of *Field & Stream* that was left. When she finally asked if anyone cared to pass time in the lab before her . . . well, to say she received enthusiastic encouragement to leave would be putting it mildly.

Kurt grimaced back at her, *not* a devout morning person—though come to think of it, his night hadn't been all that good either, thanks to her. She'd left him with a thousand questions and no answers. He'd hardly slept a wink.

"Well, now that you're here, pull up a chair and don't talk to me," he said. "I'm busy."

"With what?" she asked.

The question was made to sound innocent enough, but he knew better. She knew better, too, so he ignored her.

She sighed and scraped a chair across the floor to sit at a small empty worktable. She sighed again—nothing to do. She coughed and scratched her leg, then picked up a company memo regarding paper waste and assigned-parking infractions and read it. She put it down. She picked it up again and made a paper airplane out of it.

That done, she smoothed out her thick, straight-as-a-board brown hair and scratched her leg again, inspecting the sight for a bug bite. Nothing. But she could use a manicure—her mother would have a fit if she could see how short and ill-shaped her nails were. Her cuticles were a disaster.

"Do you ever listen to music in here?" she asked.

He sighed laboriously, then looked at her. He lowered his eyes and swallowed a chuckle of the frustration, not humor variety, when she immediately changed her expression to that of a pathetic dimwit with nothing to do. When he could look at her again, he pointed to a small portable radio on top of the incubator. The only thing he ever listened to was the news in the morning; the radio belonged to the maintenance man.

"Thanks," she said, feigning humble gratitude. "I really appreciate this. Thank you. So much."

He aligned his eyes to the microscope once more, but he couldn't see anything. With his peripheral vision he was watching her walk with slow easy grace, and wondering why he hadn't noticed how long and shapely her legs were—that was generally one of the first things he noticed about a woman. But the day before she hadn't been a woman, she'd been a pest. She was still a pest, he decided, focusing his eyes on a healthy young colony of saprophytes from which he'd taken several DNA samples to graft to those of other bacteria during the creation of A-B1.

The fine sweet strains of a classical piece by Haydn was easy to adjust to, and it acted as a barrier between him and the pest and her constant breathing and moving. If he couldn't concentrate on the slide, the music would remind him to refocus, being far less distracting than she was. . . .

But the loud thumping of the country music she chose sent him straight up the wall.

"No, no, no. Absolutely not," he said, shouting to be heard. "How do you expect me to think through that racket?"

"You don't like country music?"

"Not that loud!"

"It's meant to be played loud."

"No. Not even faintly. No, I don't like country music," he decided more decisively.

She was no great country-western fan herself, but for this sort of reaction from the great Dr. Andropov, she could pretend to be almost anything.

"How can you not like country music? America *is* country music. It's what life in America is all about."

"Not my life, so find something else." He turned back to the scope—marking an end to their country-music conversation.

A local country/rock station got her the same glare of disapproval, and straight rock and roll had him off his stool and marching across the room to relocate the classical station.

The whole incident made her laugh. Bugging him was more fun than taking a bag full of snakes to an Avon party.

"That's going to put me to sleep," she grumbled, heading back to her chair with a good sense of how far far-enough was. He raised his eyebrows as if to say, So go to sleep. "You're not being very hospitable."

He ignored her, readjusting himself on the stool.

She crossed her legs, swinging one foot, but it had more to do with releasing pent-up energy than keeping time with Chopin. She braced her head on her elbow for a while, then lowered her arms and her head to the table-top with a groan.

He cleared his throat harshly at her.

She knew for a fact that he wasn't paying any attention to her—because she was watching him. He hadn't shaved again that day and he was looking pretty rugged. A little Tom Sellick-y in one of those out-on-the-prairie-for-days-and-days westerns. His dark hair was clean and shiny, and the gray at the temples made her wonder exactly how old he was—late thirties, early forties? And what about a wife and children? She probably should have wondered about that before. He wasn't wearing a ring, which didn't mean anything, but he also hadn't said anything about them—and men always talk about their children, if not their wives, eventually.

Of course, it didn't really matter—which was probably why she hadn't wondered about it before. She could hardly stand him, he was so arrogant and selfish and nasty. He really wasn't worth thinking about. At all.

The memo-plane she'd constructed earlier was a huge temptation . . . one she resisted over and over until it overwhelmed her. Her fingers crawled across the table until she could hold it between her thumb and index finger, testing its weight and size. She was pretty sure she was only going to get one shot at flying it, so she needed to make it count. Snatching a pen from a glass with several others in it, she scribbled a note on the wing and took careful aim.

Cupping his left hand along the side of his face as if it were a blinder on a plow horse, he found he could actually pretend she wasn't there for whole minutes at a time. Once or twice he imagined he could smell her, and he'd look up quickly to see if she was on the prowl.

Odd. He wasn't the least bit startled when a green airplane landed on the counter in front of him. Without moving his head, his eyes tracked it as it skidded to a stop near his right hand. *Un*amused, he admired her skills as a pilot, but didn't move or say a word. It wasn't until he noticed the message on the wing—*I'M SO BORED*—that it became necessary for him to bite down hard on his inner cheeks and squelch the bubbling urge to laugh.

It didn't work. He started laughing, his superiority weakened by half, his reserve severely breached.

She got up and took a step or two forward, smiling, mighty pleased with her accomplishment. Making him laugh was nice. Making him roar with glee was even finer.

He nodded, grinning, chuckling weakly. "I'm sorry you're bored, Doctor. I really am. Have you thought of reading a good book or catching up on correspondence—I rarely mail anything anymore, but I understand many people still do and that women are especially deft at penning notes to one another."

Another slur on her gender—an insult that was more than skin deep, that went beyond any alleged defects in her character. An attack on biological grounds was really dirty pool.

Too bad she was on the begging end of this discussion.

"Please," she said, exaggerating her whine. "Let me do something. Anything. Wash petri dishes. Scrub the floors with a toothbrush. Filing. I have a great recipe for agar. I can do cultures. I know lab procedures. I can . . . Oh, I know, I can work on whatever you were working on before Andropov-B went berserk," she said, eager and hopeful. "No offense, of course. In fact, I'll make you a deal. If you give me something to do, I won't interfere with your A-B1 experiments for the duration of the quarantine. Unless, of course, you ask for my help, and then I'd be glad to offer any assistance I can. And . . . and naturally, once the quarantine is lifted, all deals are off, but just think of all the time I could save you. I'll work from your notes—I bet you make great notes—and you wouldn't even have to stop and explain it to me. I'm a quick study. Truly. I graduated fourth in my class. I wanted to graduate first, to drive my mother insane with a daughter who turned out to be a . . . a dark navy blue stocking, but . . . well, I did the best I could and it wasn't half-bad and I do good work. If you'd just give me something to do . . ."

"Gram-stain the blood samples in the fridge," he said, before turning back to his work.

No please or howdy-do, but she wasn't going to quibble over it.

For the next few hours they worked companionally if silently together in the lab, save some of the best pieces of classical music ever written, of course. And he didn't even seem to mind that she hummed some-times—though she'd catch herself at it and stop immediately, not wanting him to fly into the fluorescent lighting again.

After lunch she became moderately interested in helping Dwayne with the Empire State Building. His attention span—as a new nonsmoker—was a little short. He'd never finish it if someone didn't help him. But she still had several dishes of cultures to stain and label, so she left the door to the lab open, and when the young man would come to the doorway waving his arms to get her attention, she'd leave to help him for a minute or two.

Sometime before dinner, Kurt glanced across his lab at the small worktable where Mack and Dwayne had their heads together, finishing their damned puzzle. Joanne, too, had taken a turn at soothing Dwayne's nicotine nerves and was now in his greenhouse misting the plants with a water bottle—attempting to save and repair her own nerves, no doubt. He could hear Polly in the next room, through the open door, snoring loud enough to make him believe a convoy of tractor trailers was driving through his waiting room.

He wanted to cry.

Don't ask how it happened, he didn't know.

Looking back, he supposed it was easier to let her come and go in the lab than to hold his breath, maintaining rigid control of himself every time she came within two feet. He was so afraid he'd start talking to her; look at her and be unable to look away; reach out and touch her—and then what?

"If you stay up to watch *Real Cops* tonight, you might be able to see what she looks like," Dwayne was telling Mack, the puzzle once again forgotten.

"Myrna was arrested? On television?" She sounded shocked for some reason. It was Kurt's guess that

Dwayne was driving at the time and would also be a featured guest on the program.

"Nah. She did a gig for 'em. You know, the reenactment part? When they do the Arizona cops, they use local Arizona actors for the TV show. It's cheaper that way. Myrna's thinking of going to Hollywood in a couple of years. She wasn't too interested in acting till she got this bit, but the director said she had real potential and should keep up the good work."

"And she'll be on TV tonight?" Mack made it sound like something worth living for.

"Well, we don't know for sure. We've been watching every night. They never give you specific dates. They say within the next six months or sometime in October . . . stuff like that."

"Is anyone hungry other than me?" Kurt asked, walking up behind them, placing his hand lightly on the back of Dwayne's neck. He was checking Dwayne's temperature, of course, but the boy seemed to think it some gesture of affection, for he looked up and smiled at Kurt with great fondness. Kurt smiled back. "We're going to have to complain if they're planning to serve us this late every night. It's nearly seven-thirty."

"You're kidding. Really?"

Kurt found it hard to believe they'd been so absorbed in the puzzle that they'd forgotten to get hungry—even the aerobic bacillus he'd spent the afternoon with wasn't *that* interesting.

Nor could he believe the lack of conscience they were exhibiting at the invasion of his lab. Not a guilty expression anywhere. Even that pesky bug of a Southern belle now looked as if she owned the place, rubbing shoulders with the boy, her feet propped on a chair and crossed at the ankles; laughing and smiling as if she were his older sister.

Clearly she was old enough to be his much older sister—his mother, if she'd married extremely young. And if he thought for a second she could be interested in a dolt like Dwayne, he might almost be jealous.

No, not jealous. Skeptical. Appalled.

Still, it was beyond him what she saw in Dwayne as a brother or a son or even a pal. She wasn't that relaxed in *his* presence, didn't laugh or talk as much—unless it was to say something calculated to irritate him.

"Ah, there's your supper now, Doctor," Mack said, getting up when she heard the hall door opening. "I better wake Polly before she scares them away."

"Man, have you ever heard an old lady snore like that before?" Dwayne asked him.

"I don't believe so, no." Kurt hadn't listened to *that* many women sleep, come to think of it. His mother, a few one-night stands in college, his ex-wife, a few short entanglements since then . . . he wondered if Mack snored. Or would she curl up and purr?

"Can't we eat first?" he heard her saying, talking to someone who'd just come in. "We're all starving."

Kurt and Dwayne joined Mack and Polly in the waiting room, Dwayne calling to Joanne to come and eat. A space-suited employee was attaching a small box to the telephone on Joanne's desk and there was no food in sight.

"What's happening here?" he asked, assuming he was still leader of the pack. "Do you have any idea what time it is?"

"Sorry, Doc," the man mumbled through his mask, turning all the way around to look at him through his plastic window. "Food's outside, and we'll bring it in as soon as we can, but you wouldn't believe what's been going on out there today." Kurt couldn't believe what had happened in his lab today! "Some voodoo woman called the TV station this morning, insisting that she predicted that a disaster was going to happen here yesterday and gave them the whole story. We put them off as long as we could, but it was all over the news early this afternoon." Eyes slowly gravitated in Dwayne's direction. "Dr. Preston heard about it in Texas and flew back straightaway, and he wants to talk to all of you," he said, holding up a speakerphone. "And the Centers for Disease Control heard about it; they want all sorts of written reports and—"

"And we want our dinner," Kurt said, hungry and more than a little annoyed by the whole thing. "You tell Dick Preston that we'll talk after we've eaten. And you can handle the CDC, that's what you get paid to do. Have you informed them yet that Dr. McKissack is involved?"

"Not yet, sir. I said three doctors and two laypeople. They didn't seem to care *who* it was as long as they got their forms filled out."

Kurt nodded. "I understand. Bureaucrats. Fax me everything before you send it to them, will you?"

"Yes, sir."

"Now then, if you'll get them to start passing in the food, you can hook up that little box while we're eating, take our blood and vital signs while we're talking to Dr. Preston, and be done with us for the day," he said, organizing the man's life for him.

"Don't you just love a take-charge man?" Polly asked. "My Drew was the same way. Sure as gravity, he always knew what to do. My Drew."

Unobtrusively, Kurt moved to the wall behind Mack and leaned against it to wait.

"You should probably call the office before those reports go in," he said in a voice too low to be heard through the rear of a space suit.

"I was thinking the same thing, thanks. And think how grateful our spaceman will be when I start sending my own reports—in triplicate—from the inside."

"Think he'll be grateful enough to smuggle us in a pizza?" he asked, catching the first distinct aromatic waves of cafeteria food.

"I work for CDC, remember? I know them. He'll be so grateful, we'll be eating steaks from Black Angus."

They grinned at each other—accidentally—their eyes meeting on a level that was as close as two people could get without actually touching. Camaraderie. They continued to smile when they looked away, off balance, feeling a little reckless.

"Dick," Kurt said, a short while later. He was holding a cotton ball in the bend of his arm and resting his ankle comfortably on his opposite knee as if he were about to have a chat with an old school chum. "How was Texas?"

"Big," came a smoky voice over the speakerphone. "And in dire need of more fertilizer, if you can believe it. You'd think they'd be knee-deep in it by now, the way they go on down there."

"You should be glad they're not."

"Somewhere in my heart I am," Preston said with a Texas drawl that was thick enough to stand a flagpole in. "You know I am. I just can't help wishin' the company had diversified into plastics when they had the chance.

Between you and the damned nature lovers with their moanin' and groanin' about pollution, I can see myself going out of business here before too long."

"You'll pull some other miracle out of your hat before that happens," Polly said, reassuring him with a soundless snap of her fingers.

"Polly? That you? How are you feelin', old girl?"

"Oh, Dick, I'm just fine."

"Who's watchin' your cats?"

"Little Lucy Miller from down the street. So sweet. She always watches them for me when I'm away. They just love her. And she's so good with them. Doesn't put up with any nastiness from the boys, and all the girls are in before dark."

"Good. Good." Preston paused. "Kurt?" There was an odd, cautioning note in his voice. One his employee seemed to understand.

"I'm keeping my end of the deal, Dick, so it'll be a while yet before you have to pack up for the poorhouse."

"Not if you keep pulling these damned stupid stunts like this one yesterday, it won't. First we get those fools in Atlanta down our throat about A-B1, and now this. What the hell happened?"

Dwayne squirmed uncomfortably beside him. No one put killing for a cigarette beyond his capabilities just then.

"To the fools in Atlanta? Or what happened yesterday?" Kurt asked, smiling.

There was a long pause. "Are you there, Dr. McKissack?" Dick Preston asked.

"Yes, Doctor," Mack said, also smiling.

"Well, I don't know you personally, so I don't know if you fit the description, but I've been dealing with some of your colleagues today, and there are some that are . . . none too savvy."

"Yes, Doctor. I understand. It sometimes happens in large organizations. Myself, I've been dealing with two of *your* colleagues for two days now. One is an intelligent charming hospitable woman, and the other is . . . Dr. Andropov. I'd have to say we're about even on that score."

A belly-rumbling guffaw echoed through the room from the speakerphone box. "Well, hold my nose and call me fat, I think you got a live one there, Kurt."

"Unquestionably." Kurt glanced at Mack briefly, but it was long enough to see the sassy grin on her lips and the merry light in her eyes and to feel his body grow taut with desire. He did enjoy a feisty female.

"So what the hell happened yesterday? If you'll excuse my language, ladies."

Dwayne took in a deep breath and held it, waiting for that dreaded moment of responsibility to come around once again. In the back of his mind he stood blindfolded before a firing squad smoking a cigar-sized cigarette. He was prepared to accept all the blame.

"To tell you the truth, Dick," Kurt said. "The closest I've come to figuring out what happened yesterday . . . well, it can be said in three simple words."

Everyone waited for the words.

"Which three words?" Dick finally asked.

"Friday the thirteenth. Dick, that accident was going to happen somewhere yesterday. It just happened to happen here." Kurt turned his head and winked at Dwayne, who beamed at him.

"Are you out of your mind?"

"No, sir. If you'd taken the time to check, you'd have discovered that there are stars completely out of sync with this planet. Pieces of karma are missing. There's a spiritual transmigration going on here that's . . . that's bigger than all of us. Whatever happened yesterday couldn't have been stopped."

There was an enormous pregnant pause.

"You're not going to tell me what happened," Dick said, and he wasn't guessing.

"That's as good as it gets, Dick, unless one of the others can explain it better."

Nope. No. That was pretty much it, all right.

Dwayne opened his mouth to speak, and Polly put a finger to it, shaking her head.

"Say, Dick," Kurt said, chuckling quietly. "Do you think you could round us up a VCR and some movies? Daytime television is impossible to follow. Turned out Roy was having an affair with his own grandmother this afternoon and—"

"It was his aunt, dear," Polly corrected him.

"What movies do you want?" Dick asked, getting the picture too clearly.

Okay. So he wasn't completely obnoxious, she decided, taking an occasional, covert glance at Kurt as the five of them put off going to bed, fearing they'd miss Myrna's acting debut on *Real Cops*. Frankly, she would have slit her wrists before she missed the program.

Of course, her motives were based on pure curiosity. Kurt's reputation would preclude his doing anything he didn't want to do, number one. And number two, his obvious lack of attention to the present program and the extraordinary amount of frivolous small talk he was exchanging with the others was looking more and more like goodwill.

Oops. He caught her sneaking a peek at him, and she looked away.

It would be just her luck to be falling in love with someone like him—a halfway decent man under layers and layers of pomposity and gall—as if she didn't have enough to contend with in life.

Love? No, no, not love. She hadn't meant to think that. There were no choirs of angels or bells ringing here. It was dislike at first sight, right? Extreme physical attraction, that's all it was. His few good points were so outnumbered by the bad ones . . . No, no, no. Not love. And being attracted to someone and acting on it were two very different things, she reminded herself, looking up to find his gaze on her.

He didn't look away—so rude—but then, neither did she. She liked looking at him. It gave her an airy feeling in her chest that made everything seem big and wondrous; full of possibilities. She imagined his touch to be alarmingly gentle and intuitive; his kisses to be long and deep; his body hard and demanding. . . .

"Are you feeling ill, dear," Polly asked. Sitting next to her, it was a simple matter for the old lady to reach up and feel Mack's forehead with the back of her hand. "You look a little flushed."

"Do I?" Mack said, averting her eyes, putting both hands to her cheeks. They were fire hot on the inside, but cool enough to the touch. How strange.

Kurt looked away, closing his eyes for a brief moment of solitude. What *was* he doing? What makes a man put himself through this? he wondered, wanting her with every fiber of his being. Was her hair any softer than any other woman's? Her eyes brighter? *Why* would he want another woman in his life? And why this one? he pondered, succumbing to the inevitable—to a fascination with this particular woman that he wouldn't be able to ignore as he had so many others.

He was no boy. And she wasn't the sort of woman he'd choose as a mild distraction. What *was* he doing? And why couldn't he stop it? Would a sane man be wondering what made her tick? Would he care if she was bored or happy or depressed or tired? Would he say quick short prayers to whoever was listening for her continued good health; for one of her smiles; for a chance at her affections? Was there an emotional death wish built into the Y-chromosome that compelled a man to throw caution to the wind when all his best instincts told him otherwise?

It was a question worthy of another Kingsford research grant, he was sure.

"Doctor, I glanced at a few of the slides you made today. They looked good," Kurt said, trying to imagine—among other things—what he'd do without his lab for two weeks. "I was wondering if you'd be interested in classifying them for me tomorrow."

She looked at him. A first-year microbiology student can stain tissues and cells to facilitate study and identification. Had he really expected her work to be anything other than perfect? And why the sudden generosity in sharing his lab?

"I'm particularly interested in the gram-negative bacilli," he said, when she sat staring at him suspiciously as if he were trying to trick her. "I believe it's the cause of a bovine bacteremia, a rather severe bloodstream infection in cows. It . . . it's almost never preventable, being part of the animal's natural bacterial flora, but I believe it's curable."

"And it has nothing to do with A-B1," she said. It was

something to do, but not what she came for. Mercy work.

"No," he said, astonished that he was feeling something akin to guilt for sticking to his guns. He knew what she wanted so badly to work on, but no one knew the Andropov-B bacteria better than he did. And too much was at risk.

As for Mack, she wasn't sure if she was feeling insulted or ingenious. It was another milestone in her scheme to become involved with the A-B1 investigation. It was an act of trust on his part and nothing to spit at.

"I'll do my best, Doctor. Thank you," she said. Her cheeks were burning again.

They featured the South Dakota cops that night, and only Dwayne and Kurt remained up to watch the show to the end.

Mack was still awake when the light under the door went out. She was sitting up in her cot with her back against the wall an hour later, knowing she couldn't get up and wander about without waking the others—most particularly Kurt, as he was probably sleeping on the couch in the waiting room and would hear her even if she kept to the lab, the only unoccupied room at night.

Over and over she'd find the most comfortable place on the cot and lie staring at the darkness, her body exhausted, her mind unable to shut down. What should she do about the lust she saw lurking in Kurt's lingering glances? Was hers as obvious? She didn't have a legal will. Should she write something out or just hope her mother got everything? What would it be like to kiss him? Who'd clean out her office? Wouldn't it be lovely to have him lying close to her and to smell that musky-soapy smell all she wanted? To feel his warm skin slide beneath her fingertips? When would they deliver her suitcase from the hotel? She should check on that, first thing in the morning. Would he roll over and fall asleep or hold her until morning? Would he talk or grunt or be stoic? Would he be gentle or rough? If they gave her job to that twerp, Ed Goldbloom, in national statistics she'd have to haunt the CDC. What would happen to them when the quarantine was lifted? Would he brush her off, ask her to stay, follow her home, or send her postcards for a month or two before he forgot her?

Her last glance at the clock told her it was four in the morning; her mind did a slow jog through that half-asleep state of wild imaginings. Kurt made wild sweet love to her, made her heart pound and excitement churn low in her abdomen, then he took her to a party—a "Celebration of Life" that looked more like a New Year's Eve party. There were no strangers. . . .

SIX

The blood samples had been taken randomly from a large herd of cows in Utah. The gram-negative bacillus Mack was looking for was present in every sample in varying degrees—something she and Kurt had expected to see. She spent the morning dividing the samples into three groups. Healthy cows with a low number of the gram-negative bacillus in their bloodstream naturally; those with a marked increase—something that could happen naturally or could be an indication of early infection; and those with a decidedly high number of bacillus and clearly diseased.

Later, cultures of the bacillus would be made and the long arduous process of testing various known and new antibiotics, chemicals, vitamins, and minerals on the cultures would begin, in search of a safe, affordable cure. Since the bacillus was part of the natural flora of the animal and served a purpose, whatever cure was developed for the disease couldn't destroy the bacteria completely—that would make the cure as deadly as the disease. It was all very tricky and interesting, and what she loved about the profession.

"You're up early," Kurt said, not two feet away, though she hadn't heard him enter the room, absorbed as she was in a foreign microworld.

"What? Yes. I am." And had been since the first rays of light from the windows of the greenhouse had shown her the way around the lab. Since then she'd been working quietly with the aid of a lamp and the light of the microscope. "I haven't missed breakfast, have I?"

"No," he said, frowning. "How long have you been in here?"

"I haven't touched anything but the slides I prepared yesterday," she said, feeling nervous and defensive—and not about her work. "You said I could do this, remember?"

"Of course, but I didn't mean it had to be done before breakfast."

She smiled. "Oh. Well, I woke up early and—"

"Did Polly's snoring wake you up?"

"No." She laughed. "Could you hear her? Did she wake you up?"

"No, I . . . Is your cot uncomfortable?"

"What are you, the sleep police? Is waking up early a crime?"

"No. But you couldn't get to sleep the night before and . . ."

"I see," she said, and only half teasing, she added, "You think I'm a crazed insomniac who might screw up your slides or sneak over and mess with your tests on Andropov-B."

He thought she was as crazy as a blue goose, but that was all.

"I'm sure you're too proud and too stubborn to do

either of those things, Doctor. I'm merely concerned that you might have forgotten that lack of sleep lowers your resistance to infection. So, if Polly's snoring or the cot are keeping you awake, you should ask your friend Eugene for a better bed and/or a set of earplugs."

At his look of concern and the crushed animation in his voice, she felt like a heel.

"Polly and the cot aren't nearly as bad as some I've actually gotten used to in places like Ghana and Laos and Botswana," she said, much less defensive. "I slept in a hut once, next to a man who could actually move the dirt back and forth on the floor between us with his snoring. Polly's an amateur."

"You must see a great many interesting things in your travels," he said, envying her that part of her job. He'd inherited a small portion of his father's wanderlust, but had never had much of a chance to do anything about traveling, aside from vacations. "Me, I get soil samples from the places you see. Doesn't tell me much about the people."

She nodded, removing the slide from the scope and placing it with the others in the third group. "That's the best part, the part I love. That's why I took the job in the first place. I wanted to see the world. The furthest I'd ever been from Vicksburg was up the Yazoo River to Arkabutla Lake on a boating trip with my father one summer." She took another slide and slipped it under the lens. "I hated the life my mother wanted for me in Vicksburg, but I wasn't exactly cut out to be a catfish farmer either. For a long time I didn't think there was a place for me anywhere."

She put her eyes to the microscope, going silent to secure a good fix.

"Somehow I'm not making the connection between

seeing the world and developing an interest in microbiology."

"No?" she said, looking up at him, averting her eyes just as quickly when she found his gaze directed at her—and acutely intense. "The first time I looked through a microscope I was a junior in high school, and . . . well, there never was a more out-of-step-with-the-rest-of-the-world person than me." She laughed softly. "I didn't fit into my mother's world. I didn't fit in my father's world. But inside that microscope was a microworld where living things needed food to survive and some needed air, while others died in the presence of oxygen. They colonized and reproduced. Some were unpredictable, almost as if they had a personality. Later, I found out that I could make a difference in their world. I introduced them to other bacteria, just to see what would happen." She removed the slide and put it with the others in the second group and took another. "I froze 'em and cooked 'em and dried 'em out. I weeded out bad ones and nourished good ones. Then I started to study the bad ones and I watched as they spread like a cancer and killed their victims. By then I was in graduate school. The pathology of microorganisms seemed like a natural next step. Studying the victim to discover which bad guy killed him." She frowned into the scope. "I didn't know cows had anaerobic parasites as part of their natural flora."

"Now you do," he said shortly. "So you thought you were a microdetective, so to speak."

"Yes," she said, looking up again, her smile stopping his heart. "I went to work at CDC, and after a few dull years in a lab doing routine work, they gave me a badge and some authority. Finally I had some power in my life," she said comically, rubbing her hands together.

"And they wanted me to travel. Hunt bad guys to the ends of the earth and back if I had to; put an end to their reign of death and destruction."

"And how long ago was that?"

"Almost ten years."

"And you never get tired of the traveling?"

She hesitated. "I didn't say that."

"So, you are tired of it?"

"No. A little maybe. Some." She looked into the microscope, flustered and confused. "I love to travel. I've seen so much. I've . . . I've learned so many things."

"But?"

She shook her head without looking up. "No buts."

But she didn't have anyone to call who'd miss her in two weeks' time. *But* she was tired and lonely. *But* she was never in one place long enough to make close friends or have a decent relationship. *But* she still didn't fit in anywhere, except when her mind was inside the tiny world under a microscope.

"You must be going nuts stuck here in one place," he said empathetically.

"I've been stuck in places before. Sometimes it takes months to track down carriers. When the AIDS virus first broke out in rural Chile, one of the carriers was a traveling salesman who went from one small village to the next selling pots and pans, and infecting almost every young girl who'd sleep with him." Movement in the next room caught her attention. She grinned at him. "Sounds like breakfast."

They said little more as they tidied up and joined the others for their morning meal. And for the rest of the day no opportunity for private conversation presented itself, with the others coming and going at will, Mack deeply into the microworld she loved so much, and Kurt . . . deeply into Mack.

He couldn't count the times he caught himself watching her hands. In repose they were calm, steady, and artwork perfect. They moved with the grace of butterflies, flitting across a field of wildflowers. He liked the way she bent her head over the microscope, her hair falling forward on both sides, exposing the nape of her neck where her skin looked soft and pale and inviting.

She was diligent, and he liked that too. One of those people with the gift of tuning out the world while she worked. Dwayne had to call her name more than once to get her attention.

It amused him that despite all her best efforts to resist it and contrary to what she imagined, a great deal of her mother's frivolous polish and refinement had rubbed off on her. She was very much female.

"Oh! My suitcase. My suitcase," she cried joyfully when it entered on the arm of the moon man at lunch. "Oh, Larry, thank you. Tell Eugene I love him. Oh, my suitcase."

She was on the floor beside it, unzipping the lid, throwing it back and rummaging through her belongings as if they were lost treasures.

"Look, Polly, electric curlers," she said, holding them up as if they were bejeweled. Joanne's parents had sent a blow dryer for Joanne's short bouncy hair, but it only straightened Mack's hair more and made Polly look like Einstein's sister. "We can do our hair. And make up. Real shampoo." Kurt could tell she was excited to see her panties and bras, but she didn't say anything. She wadded something small and silky close to her chest and held it there. He wanted to see it. "Oh, here's that sweatsuit I told you about, Polly. It might be a little big, but it'll be more comfortable than sleeping in these scrubs." She said nothing about her other clothes. She wouldn't wear them while the rest of them wore scrubs, he knew. Joanne had done the same thing with the clothes her parents had sent. Strange species, women. Strange and admirable in so many ways. "Ah! An emery board! Kurt, I'm taking the afternoon off. We girls are going to the beauty parlor."

This didn't exactly fit into his "diligent" description of her earlier, but he was too distracted to protest. She'd called him by name for the first time and . . . he liked it, the way she filled the *U* in his name with sweet Southern honey. He played it back over and over in his mind, and before he could think of a way to get her to say it again, they were gone.

They were as gone as they could be for the rest of the afternoon.

He could have shrugged such behavior off as silly, but the truth was, one particular silly female in the trio was making him feel very silly himself, and very male. He wanted to go with her, watch her excitement; observe the strange exotic feminine things she'd do to herself.

He tried to get some work done, but the giggles and whispers and padding of bare feet from the other side of his office door finally got to him. He was a decisive man by nature. Once made, his decisions were irrevocable. And, it seemed, he'd come to a decision about Mack.

"I can't take any more of this," he told Dwayne abruptly, picking up the phone for a quick call to Dick Preston. "If we don't do something about this, we'll regret it. Forever."

SEVEN

YOU ARE CORDIALLY INVITED
TO JOIN US FOR COCKTAILS
IN THE SOLARIUM AT SIX

The note slipped under the door and skidded several feet across the tiled floor a little after four that afternoon. Joanne was combing out Polly's gray fuzzy hair, and Mack was at the other end of old lady, finishing her pedicure in Paler Than Pink lacquer, much to Polly's delight.

"What's this now?" Mack asked, crawling the few feet to the note. "Keep 'em spread out, Polly, they're still tacky." She laughed. "Look at this. We're invited to cocktails in the solarium at six."

"Cocktails?" Joanne frowned. "But I thought . . ."

"Oh my, oh me, those boys are up to some fun is all, dear. They know we can't have alcohol with the medications we're taking. None at all. Gracious me, I can't remember the last time I was asked out on a date."

"Me either," Mack muttered, getting to her feet, surprised to find herself thrilled. Kurtsevo Andropov was a fountain of surprises. "And we don't even have to worry about what to wear." They laughed. Lifting Polly's face to hers with two fingers below her double chin, she smiled wickedly. "We do look good enough to eat, girl-friend."

"Girlfriend. Ha! This has been such good fun. Son of a gun, I feel like a young girl getting ready for a sock hop."

"A what?" Joanne asked.

Polly and Mack looked at each other and laughed once more. It wasn't the first time the difference in their ages had proved to be worlds apart. Polly could remember the past as if it were yesterday; Mack was old enough to remember some of it, or recall her mother telling many of the same stories. And Joanne . . . well, she provided an education on the social mores of *modern* American youth. And yet, all three generations had so much in common that the bond between them became something very real and unbreakable.

Maybe it was knowing they could die together that solidified their friendship. Maybe it was simply their sex. Mack didn't care. She felt close to Polly and Joanne. Like mother, daughter, and younger sister.

She couldn't help wondering why things couldn't have been different between her and her mother . . . She found herself missing her anyway. Briefly.

They sat on their cots waiting for the digital clock on the desk to drop the six and two zeros. They were styled, curled, and painted to perfection. Kurt's office smelled like a drugstore perfume counter. They were wearing clean cotton socks instead of the thongs they'd been given, and Mack had broken into her small stash of jew-elry—gold hoop earrings for herself, a bracelet and set of small antique marcasite earrings for Joanne, and a string of pearls with matching clusters for her ears, suited Polly very well. The three women looked at one another, bright-eyed and smiling as they rose to their feet.

"I love the way champagne tickles my nose," Polly said, ready to pretend she was Cinderella. "But, my gracious me, it goes straight to my head . . . and my toes. Promise you'll only let me drink one glass, if that's what they serve tonight. And hors d'oeuvres. I'm so hungry I could eat a million little pigs in blankets."

"A true lady will nibble at only one canapé, the second or third time the tray is passed to her. For politeness' sake only," Mack recited in a deeply Southern drawl that had her new friends in stitches. "The remains of which will be tucked inside the napkin and held in one's left hand until such time as it can be unobtrusively disposed of. This, ladies, will alleviate any worries the young lady might have at being caught in the unfortunate position of having parsley"—Joanne opened the door to the lab. Kurt and Dwayne were waiting—"stuck to her teeth."

If they'd gone to great lengths with their appearance, the gentlemen had gone further.

Over clean scrubs they wore starched white lab coats buttoned down the front, with neckties knotted loose about their bare throats. Their hair was clean, with every strand in place, *and* they'd shaved.

Dwayne stepped forward like a Royal Swiss Guard, thrusting his elbow into the air between him and Joanne, who giggled and took his arm. He smiled and stood a little taller, as if she made him feel bigger somehow, hanging on his arm, looking nervous and shy.

Shaking his head at them, Kurt stepped forward with considerably more ease, though no less formality, and offered his arm first to Age and then to Beauty.

"Ladies. Your servant," he said as they took his arm in turn. The look he gave Polly was amused and affectionate. The expression he turned to Mack was . . . not. It wasn't that she was any more beautiful than before—although she was definitely that. But he was realizing that he'd been missing her all afternoon. He cringed at the inane idea of it, but it was, nevertheless, true.

He liked having her where he could see her, where he could hear her talking, listen to her partial half-hidden drawl to his heart's content. He resisted an urge to check himself for fever. He was infected with something, but the symptoms weren't those of a diseased body. On the contrary, he'd never felt healthier.

"My, my, you look very smart in that tie, Kurt dear," Polly was saying. Reluctantly, he turned his attention to her. "Is it new?"

"I hope so. It's Dick's." Of course, they all knew that the tie, along with so many other things, would eventually be destroyed during or after the quarantine, so this was mildly amusing. "And Eugene donated his for the boy. Rather natty, don't you think?"

"You shaved."

It was an obvious statement, but the only thing Mack could think of. Moments were passing in slow motion. The desire-filled gazes Kurt directed at her couldn't possibly be lasting more than a second or two, but his eyes would meet hers, study them, look deeper and deeper until she knew he was seeing the need she was feeling. An interminable period of war between her mind and her heart would ensue and a certain satisfaction would come to light his eyes; make her feel weak and helpless against him.

Controlling herself was something she knew how to do. She did. Her heart had had yearnings before—to do unladylike things such as slouch in a chair or chew bubble gum; to associate with undesirable but very interesting people; to shirk social and familial responsibilities. Controlling herself was the key to harmony and happiness. The few times she'd allowed her heart to override her mind she'd either impulsively courted disaster or planned it so well, it became a completely controlled statement of her independence. She was *not* a weak and helpless person.

She curbed the urge to check herself for fever. She was certainly infected with something, but the symptoms weren't those of a diseased body. On the contrary, she'd never felt healthier.

"You shouldn't have shaved for this," she said quietly, lowering her gaze from the intense heat of his. She felt as if a jungle full of wild animals was caught inside her skin, prowling around, leaping, scratching, looking to be liberated. "It's not worth the risk of infection."

"Had I known it would concern you, I'd have done it sooner," he said in a tone for her ears only. Then a little louder he added, "It was a minimal risk and well worth it. I made Dick give up his electric shaver. It's not as smooth a shave as I would have liked. . . ." Leaving whisker burns on her clear pale skin would have to be recorded as a necessary evil, he was afraid. "But it's the best I could do."

"Heavenly days, your worst is better than most men's best. Isn't that so, dear?" Polly asked, bending forward to peer around Kurt at her. "Better than the rest?"

"Yes" got stuck in her throat, so she bobbed her head silently.

"You are too kind," he said, the tone of his voice lighter than before. "And may I say that I've never seen the two of you looking lovelier?"

It was another one of those over-the-rainbow, past-the-sun, around-the-moon, across-heavy-traffic, compliments he was so good at—as he'd seen her looking her normal best for only five minutes of their entire acquaintance—and still her cheeks blazed with self-conscious fire when he looked at her.

Dwayne had pushed the door of the greenhouse open for Joanne and was still holding it open for them when they arrived. It was a relief to be able to remove her hand from Kurt's arm, but while he permitted Polly to precede him through the doorway, he took Mack's hand and led her through.

She felt a thousand tickling prickles run up her arm before it went numb. Under other circumstances, his touch might have seemed innocent, accidental, even serendipitous—and to jerk her hand away would have been uncivil. As it was, the encounter was positively bold and provocative—and to jerk her hand away was . . . impossible.

The solarium had been swept and cleaned, and a card table with a white sheet tablecloth had been set up on the end closest to the lab, away from the planting troughs and cots. Some of the bigger plants had been moved closer to form an enclosure, so that if one didn't look too closely or too far beyond them, it looked like a little private garden.

Mack felt cold and alone when Kurt's grip slackened and he released her to open a ginger ale bottle he'd taken off the table. He poured clear bubbly golden fluid into each of the five champagne glasses beside it.

"In case you're wondering where everything came from," Kurt said, glancing from one astonished female face to the next, "let me say that our friend Dick Preston has five children and understands things such as this."

"Such as what?" Dwayne asked as if he hadn't been there all afternoon, sweeping and shaving and tying a necktie around his throat.

"Such as special occasions," Kurt said, handing Polly a glass. "Such as marking time with the unordinary." He handed glasses to Joanne and Dwayne at the same time, then went back for the last two. "Such as an occasional odyssey of the mind," he said, looking directly at Mack, holding her glass between them. "Such as romance."

Mack could hear the plants growing in the silence. She tried to swallow, but her mouth had gone dry. She wanted to look away, wished she could laugh carelessly, but all she could do was stare at Kurt's handsome face and submit to a laser search of her soul by his eyes.

She was *not* a weak and helpless person.

"Oh my, gracious, yes," Polly said, as if nothing curious were happening under her very nose. "It's the romantics of this world who keep civilization alive. They are the dreamers and the thinkers and the doers who keep life exciting. Most exciting."

"The poets and musicians," Joanne put in helpfully, sniffing at her wine, which didn't smell like wine at all.

"I think we should toast the romantics," Polly said, lifting her glass. She waited for all five glasses to appear over the table, the last two taking several seconds longer than the others. "And Dick Preston, for helping us to make this an unordinary evening. An—"

"An extraordinary evening," Kurt added, his eyes roving toward Mack over the brim of his glass. He caught her staring at him again, and he smiled. It helped somehow, knowing that she was as amazed and overwhelmed by the forces churning between them as he was.

She felt like an idiot. The long telling glances between them were so wanton and daring—her mother would have her strung up by her thumbs if she were there. Unfortunately, Mack's wish to stop them was even weaker than her compunctions about who saw them.

She was *not* a weak and helpless person, but sometimes the effort not to be could be quite imposing.

"We got music too," Dwayne said, hurriedly finishing off his last few drops of ginger ale to perform his duty at the radio. "Doc says we have to dance too."

"Oh no," muttered Joanne shyly, clearly reluctant to do any dancing.

"Gracious me, what a fabulous idea," Polly said. "Oh! So, ah, stellar! Yes. Glenn Miller. Young man, I'll have you know that I've been known to cut quite a rug in my time."

"Oh yeah?"

"Yes. I'll show you, if you'll do me the honor . . . ?"

Dwayne gawked at her in confusion. Finally, he shrugged and looked as low as caterpillar fuzz. "Man, I'm sorry, Polly. Doc didn't teach me any of those old dances like the waltz and the jitterbug or the cut-the-rug. He wanted to see how Myrna and me dance, but then he just said to keep it slow and don't hurt anybody."

"Oh joy, I do love children," Polly said with a cackling laugh. "It's an expression, my dear boy."

And while she went on to explain how and why a rug was cut, Kurt took Mack's glass from her slack fingers and put it with his on the table. "Shall we? It is Glenn Miller, and Dwayne's going to need a visual aide, I think."

Far be it from her to deprive Dwayne of an education.

She stepped forward and placed her hand in his, her other hand high on his upper arm, and carefully kept the appropriate nine and a half inches of space between them. She tried anyway, but Kurt was having none of it. She could see he was suitably amused by the propriety, and he played along for a few minutes until they found their rhythm together, then inch by inch he pulled her closer into his embrace, until she was close enough to feel his breath against her cheek and his heart beating against her breast; until she was close enough to rest her head on his shoulder, which she did with her eyes closed and a sigh of contentment in her soul.

They didn't speak, and she tried not to look at him too often. Tried not to notice the way their bodies touched and rubbed. She didn't know the Big Band era well enough to be able to name the performers or the tunes, but the music was familiar and comforting. She felt stiff and pigeon-toed, awkward as a cow on wet ice, but Kurt didn't seem to notice. He danced like her father, easy and graceful, as if it were second nature to him. There was barely room to turn around and spit in the greenhouse, and yet he made her feel as if they were dancing in a grand ballroom.

A pained yelp from Joanne brought her eyes wide open. Polly was teaching her and Dwayne the steps of a slow waltz, and poor Joanne was bearing the brunt of the lesson. Mack smiled and closed her eyes again with the strange sensation that all was right with the world. She sighed.

"I know," Kurt murmured close to her ear. "It's nice, isn't it?"

She could have looked up quickly and pretended not to know what he was talking about. She could have. She was a good actress, and quick on her feet, remember? But she didn't. She simply nodded and hummed her agreement. Swaying slowly in his embrace was better than nice.

She indulged herself a little longer, enjoying that falling-in-love feeling that was so fleeting and rare in life. Then she felt compelled to face reality.

"We shouldn't be doing this, you know," she said, looking at him briefly, then away. He wasn't pretending anything either.

Twice he caressed her cheek with his before placing it lightly against her skin. So warm. Baby soft.

"Why not?" he asked.

"Because it's crazy."

"Too vague, Doctor. Can you be more specific?"

She wasn't sure. His hand moved up her back and down again, lingering here and there, pressing her closer to him as they rocked back and forth to the music. She felt like electrified rubber inside.

What was the question? Oh, yes . . .

"We're being delusional," she said.

He chuckled softly in her ear. It tickled. "That's a specific type of craziness, yes, but I was hoping you'd be more explicit as to *why* we shouldn't be deluding ourselves."

"You want a list?"

"Yessss." His lips buzzed the sensitive skin below her ear, and her mind went blank.

"All right, um, we could be dead in two weeks."

"*Carpe diem*, Doctor. All the more reason to delude ourselves now, don't you think?"

"And what if we survive? There'd be no future in it. You live here. I live in Atlanta."

"Are you accustomed to having your future guaranteed? Last time I checked, the future was still a crapshoot, for everyone."

"This . . . this is an emotionally desperate time for us. We're grasping at straws."

"You don't feel like straw to me." His long arm fit almost all the way around her waist. He liked that.

"We're seeing things in each other that . . . that aren't really there."

"If you're not really here, then I believe that would be an *il*lusion rather than a *de*lusion."

"Doctor." She pulled away to look at him. "We hate each other."

He grinned, and her bones turned to liquid. "If what we're feeling is hate, we should bottle it and sell it in the lobby of the United Nations building."

The others were laughing together a few feet away. They both looked.

"That's it. Lickety-split, you've got it now." Polly was waving her arms to the rhythm while Dwayne and Joanne box-stepped with exaggerated precision—all three were absorbed in the waltz and paying them no mind.

"Okay. Maybe hate was too strong a word, but you have to agree that we don't get along very well. You don't even like me."

"I like you very much," he said, his eyes locked with hers. "I like the way you fight for what's right. I like the way your mind works. I like your eyes and the way you smell and that slightly crooked incisor that shows when you smile. I like many things about you. What have I done to make you think otherwise?" She frowned and gaped and was about to start on a whole new list of complaints when he raised his brows to stop her. "Personally. Not professionally."

"What's the difference?"

He tipped his head to one side. "Are you trying to tell me you don't know the difference between what you do for a living and what you do for yourself? For pleasure? And happiness."

She was trying to tell him that she was frightened, that she couldn't recall any other man affecting her as he did. He was handsome and by far too seductive for her peace of mind; he was strong but not unbending; he was funny and interesting. She respected him, his brilliance, and his ethics. She understood his wanting to right his own wrong if A-B1 proved to be harmful; she understood that Andropov-B was as much a part of him as a child might be.

Maybe she *was* trying to tell him that the line between her personal life and her professional life wasn't very thick. Maybe she was trying to tell him she didn't know the difference anymore.

The confusion in her eyes twisted his heart, pained him, though he wasn't too sure why. It was his experience that a woman in doubt was generally the easiest woman to control, but he hadn't meant to hurt her by probing tender places. He smiled and forfeited the answer to his question by pulling her near. He hoped that resting her head on his shoulder would be as calming to her as it was to him.

He was aware of the phone ringing in the lab, but he sure as hell wasn't going to let go of her to answer it.

The curve of her neck was driving him crazy.

The room grew very quiet, almost as if they were alone. Only some slow old tune whose day had come and gone but whose melody lived on forever kept them company.

Mack was wound up tighter than a cheap clock, her heart stopping and starting just as erratically. She felt his lips low on her throat, and a soft gasp escaped her. He did it again, swirling his tongue against her skin. Instinctively, she pressed her breasts against his chest to ease the ache to be touched. Her heart slammed against the walls of her chest. Tiny sipping kisses made her tremble on loose knees, and she looked at him.

She was begging him to kiss her. Truly. He'd never seen anything like it, ever. The walls and barriers she'd spoken of moments earlier didn't exist. There was no come-hither look, no brave challenge to seduce her, no greedy sexual come-on. She was completely vulnerable to him, her eyes pleading with him to give her what she needed.

In fascinated disbelief, he bowed his head slowly, making his intentions obvious in case he was misreading her. Still dancing, he turned his back to the others to give them some privacy and then he covered her mouth with his—half expecting her to pull away and slap him.

Instead, her mouth opened to his and her tongue met his right away. Not shy, but bold. Teasing and enticing. Convulsively, his grip on her tightened, and he deepened the kiss.

The surprise and pleasure in his low groan echoed in her ears. She closed her eyes tight, as the plants around them reeled out of focus and the music became a sort of happy humming sound from her heart. Deep inside her a wild beast awoke, hungry and dangerous. She tried to warn Kurt of its existence, biting gently on his lower lip, but he was busy with a beast of his own, nipping at her ears and down her throat.

"Dwayne, dear, it's Myrna on the phone," Polly said, her voice filtering through time and space from a place they'd left far behind. Reluctant and frustrated, forehead to forehead, they prepared themselves for an intrusion. "She wants to speak with you, dear. I told her we were having a little party, but she insisted on speaking to you personally."

The mysterious cloud that had cocooned them in a world of their own lifted slowly. Mack could feel the warmth of Kurt's breath against her lips, as short and fast as her own; could feel his heart beating rapidly beneath her palm. Glancing up, she saw the fire of his passion in his eyes and braced herself to be swallowed up with desire once again.

"Dwayne? Did you hear me? I said Myrna's on the phone. She wants to speak with you."

"Oh, man." Dwayne's disgruntlment was too much to ignore. Mack and Kurt automatically turned their heads to look at him. "Would you tell her I'm busy? Tell her I'll call her back," he said, his gaze glued to Joanne's upturned face. They looked dazed, as if they were under some magical, hypnotic spell. . . .

The doctors turned to each other in unison, eyes huge with recognition and surprise, ready to giggle, and praying that they themselves hadn't looked quite so dazed.

EIGHT

The light under the door went out an hour earlier and still Mack waited, her bones stiff with inactivity as she lay awake in the dark. She couldn't remember being happier . . . or more nervous . . . or more frightened.

"Come to me later," he'd whispered as the cocktail hour came to a close and they walked back to the outer office for dinner. Great effort had been taken to make the occasion something special. White sheets covered every flat surface, and a great many flowers from the greenhouse had been cut and placed in beakers of water about the room. The desk lamp provided overall illumination, but candles burned here and there for the sake of ambience. "Polly and the kid sleep like rocks. Wait for Joanne to fall asleep, and then meet me out here. I have another surprise for you."

Oh, she just bet he did! and she flushed hot from the roots of her hair to the tips of her toes thinking about it. He laughed.

"Maybe that, too, but I really do have another surprise for you." He caught her uneasy gaze and smiled at her. "Will you come?"

"I'll try."

And she was trying.

Dinner had been excruciating. The food had tasted like bleached paper, not because it had no flavor but because all her senses were occupied elsewhere. In her thigh when his leg brushed against hers. At the tips of her fingers when they encountered his. Around the fluttering of her soul as she listened to his voice. Up and down her spine and in the pit of her stomach when their gazes met and the hunger in his eyes told her she was looking more and more like dessert to him. She'd been right about Kurt all along. He could drive a sane person crazy.

Lucky for her, he was making her crazy in a wonderful way.

But there she was, rigid as a frozen fish, unable to move.

It wasn't that she didn't want to go—she did. She'd donned her favorite emerald-green satin traveling pajamas for the occasion. She was as giddy as a kid on Christmas Eve. She knew what was awaiting her in the next room: her fondest wish, her heart's desire. Presents and treasures galore. Still, she didn't move, unsure, worried that she might not have been good enough that year. Afraid of frightening Santa Claus off before he could leave her gifts. Wondering what he'd do if she'd asked for too much that year . . .

Visions of her mother ebbed in and out of her thoughts. Never in her life had she felt more . . . akin to her; understood her so well, or wanted to talk to her so badly.

Passion was a powerful force to withstand. Especially

if all you had to battle it with was common sense and fear. And who would understand this better than her mother? What would have happened if her mother had been a stronger person? What if she hadn't been susceptible to love and romance that summer so long ago? Come to think of it, she'd hadn't ever really said she regretted it, only that it hadn't been the wisest thing she'd ever done.

Common sense in an uncommon degree is what the world calls wisdom, her mother used to quote to her—unless, of course, Mack's reasoning was logical and sound. Then she would take the other side of the argument and the quote would be, *He who thinks himself the wisest is generally the greatest fool.*

For her part, Mack thought most everything was a matter of trial and error, and no two trials ever produced the same error. She leaned to some scholar or other's philosophy that *real* wisdom was to live your life and not to get stuck with a pocket full of regrets, which made an uncommon degree of sense to her, particularly when it fit in so well with what she wanted at the time.

However . . . and wasn't there always a however? Wasn't there an exception to every rule? And wasn't every rule meant to be broken? This time she felt as if she were standing on the edge of a cliff contemplating a jump that was either just plain suicidal or . . . or some sort of magical free-floating fall into an endless abyss of excitement and happiness, and only the jump would tell which.

She'd fancied herself in love before, several times. It was a slow, methodical process. It was the building of a relationship like the Egyptians built a pyramid, one stone at a time. This time it was as if she'd passed through some invisible time barrier and found a ready-built pyramid set in place, waiting to be claimed.

If it hadn't been for the way Joanne's deep breathing and Polly's snorting synchronized and then fell apart to an uneven rhythm, then synchronized and fell apart again, she might have been there all night second-guessing herself. As it was, the preservation of her limited mental faculties required her to leave the room. But instead of sneaking into the outer office, she slipped past Polly and into the lab.

She stood there for several moments, orienting herself in the dark, squinting to see through the open door to the outer office.

"Mack?" She wasn't startled to hear Kurt's whispered voice. She was half hoping he'd be there to remove the last of the doubts she was having. "Mack? Are you there?"

Stepping toward his voice, she could barely make out his large form as he came at her, to find her in the darkness. His hands framed her face, lifted it to his mouth. She raised up on tiptoe as he kissed her, over and over, as if their hours apart had been a lifetime. Her hands pressed against his ribs, slid to his back, and pulled him close.

It had been a lifetime. Hers.

"What took you so long?" he asked, dotting her face with quick eager kisses.

"I have no idea." And she didn't. If there had been a doubt or a question in her mind, it wasn't there now. She wanted another kiss, and got one.

"I thought you might have changed your mind."

"I did," she said, kissing him again. "A hundred times."

"Mack?" he said, his voice raspy with emotion and confusion, as she settled back on her heels and held him tight about the chest. "Are you alright?" She nodded. "Is

something wrong?" She shook her head. "Mack." He
wanted her full attention. She raised her head and looked
at him, at the light and dark shadows of his face. "It's
okay, you know. Whatever you decide, it's okay. If you
want to wait until the quarantine is lifted, until life seems
a little more normal, that's fine. We can wait. If you want
to wait until I can call you on the phone and ask you out
on a date, or until I can declare my intentions toward you
to your mother, that's okay too." She squinted then,
hoping to see if he was joking. "But this is no delusion,"
he said. "What we're feeling is very real. I want you."

This was not a declaration of his undying love for her
or a promise to give her the moon and the stars. But the
profound sincerity in his voice made verbal declarations
and promises trivial and unnecessary. It held her fast,
trusting and secure in the knowledge that whatever was
his to give at that moment was hers without reserve.

Somehow, to a woman brought up to distrust im-
pulses, to require guarantees, to be prudent and wary and
to look to the future, it was more than enough. Somehow
an isolated moment of passion and abandon seemed irresistible compared with a lifetime of loneliness and carefully planned monotony.

"Mack, talk to me. What are you thinking?"

She sighed, resting her head against his chest once
more. After a moment she said, "I'm thinking that Friday
the thirteenth may have gotten a bad rap. I'm thinking it
might be a lucky day for some people."

"Like us?" he asked, a smile in his voice.

"Exactly like us," she said, letting him tip her head
back for another soul-shattering kiss.

"Come with me, I want to show you something," he
said, taking her hand abruptly and leading her toward the
greenhouse.

"What. No foreplay?"

He chuckled deep inside his chest. "Patience," he said. "Shhhh. Be very quiet."

Amazingly, it was brighter in the greenhouse than in the lab, despite the lack of light. The stars and a full moon shone down through the glass ceiling, making it perfectly easy and safe to skulk in and out of the shadows of the plants to the far end of the room, beyond the cots and the tangled lump of blankets and legs that was Dwayne sleeping.

They scooted sideways between the planting troughs, keeping their arms high to avoid disturbing anything. On the other side, Kurt pulled her down beside him into a squatting position in front of a plant-laden table and the exterior wall of glass.

He reached out to angle her head so he could whisper directly into her ear.

"When I give the signal, crawl under the table."

Mack reached out and did the same to his head. "Why?"

"Shhh. It's my surprise."

If he was dreaming that she'd make love to him under a table with Dwayne not ten feet away, he was in for a sad awakening.

He stood, and she watched as he forged his way through the thick foliage above, stretching, grunting softly until he gave a satisfied sigh and tapped her gently on the shoulder.

Filled with misgivings but game just the same, she got to her hands and knees and put her head under the table.

A cool, fresh breeze caressed her cheeks, tickled her nose, and like a curling index finger beckoned her to follow it.

"Oh. Wow!" She gasped softly, pushing at the glass door that Kurt held ajar from above. She squirmed out onto a concrete balcony, holding the door open with her backside as she looked around, openmouthed and dizzy from breathing real air.

Kurt prodded her on from behind and held his finger to his lips when she would have spoken to him. He turned back to the door, wedging a small opening with a doorstop.

Waiting for him to speak first, she let him lead her to the railing that adjoined the end of the building. She tripped over something in the shadows, and he caught her by the forearms and held her close for a moment. They were both smiling and gleeful, like two kids making a clean escape from boarding school. He leaned against the brick wall behind him, turned her around, and pulled her back against him.

"What do you think?"

Breathlessly, she shook her head in wonder at the big round moon hanging low before them, the stars like diamonds on black velvet, the long stretch of darkness that was the desert and the lights of . . . whatever town that was beyond.

"I think I fell asleep after all. I'm dreaming. I can't believe this . . . or how much I've missed fresh air." She took in a deep breath of it, lolling her head back against his shoulder. "What a lovely surprise."

"You're a lovely surprise."

She smiled. "That was the first thing you said to me, but I didn't think you really meant it." She could feel his chuckle through her back.

"But I did," he said. "I'd pictured the extremely persistent Dr. McKissack as an eight-foot Amazonian warrior with her hair in a tight knot on the top of her head, wearing yellow-tinted glasses, squeaky orthopedic shoes, and a brown wool suit, who smelled of camphor and cinnamon chewing gum. *You* were a lovely surprise."

She laughed. "Dr. McKissack wouldn't have had to be so persistent if Dr. Andropov wasn't such a spoiled brat."

"Oh, now . . . My work insists that I be a perfectionist. Can I help it if to some people I appear to be . . . demanding. Difficult at times. Temperamental if you stretch that word to mean that I expect a certain degree of excellence in those working around me. I will concede to mean, nasty, and mad as a rattlesnake when I am provoked, but I am not a spoiled brat."

"It's probably a genetic thing anyway," she went on, as if she hadn't heard him. "Something inherent to the Y-chromosome that makes men harder to get along with than women."

"Are you kidding? I am incredibly easy to get along with."

"Right."

"I am. I haven't won a single argument with you since you got off that damned elevator."

She went silent to think that one over. Turning her head to look at him, she grinned. "That's right, you haven't, have you?"

His eyes narrowed at the challenge in hers. He could see he was about to lose another skirmish if he didn't kiss her pretty soon.

"No. I haven't," he said, turning her at the waist to face him. "Which only goes to show what a misunderstood individual I am."

It was difficult to look sympathetic with her tongue in her cheek. "I'm beginning to see that," she said, holding her breath as his hands found her bare midriff, his thumbs caressed her soft, sensitive belly.

"It's a well-known fact that men who are passionate about their work tend to be passionate about everything in their lives." She had silk-covered ribs and a smooth sloping back. The smell of her was eating up his senses.

"Really? Such as?"

"Football," he said, his hands gliding forward to cover her breasts. He felt her knees buckle, and she leaned the lower half of her body against his for support. He teased her already hard nipples with the pads of his thumbs and watched as her eyes closed.

"Football . . ." she muttered.

"And politics," he said, bending her back until she exposed her neck to him. "The environment and space exploration . . ."

Kissing and nibbling his way up the column of her throat to her ear, he felt her quiver like a bowstring between his hands. The low, helpless moan from deep in her chest made his heart soar.

"Umm . . . exploration," she murmured, loosing the last tenuous hold she had on her mind, her need for him throbbing deep and low in her pelvis.

"Soft Southern accents . . . and green-eyed doctors . . ."

Her grip on his upper arms tightened. His mouth covered hers, sucking her life's breath away. Slowly. Surely. Sensuously. Instinctively she moved one of her legs to straddle one of his. She rubbed gently to ease the sweet pain, and shot a million volts of ecstasy surging through her body.

His hands slid up her body, up her arms, pushing the green satin pajama top with them, ignoring the buttons down the front. Sinking low on the wall behind him, he suckled first one breast, then the other, tugging easily at the elastic at her waist. On his knees, he scattered kisses across her abdomen, pushing the pajama bottoms to her ankles. She bent over his back to grab the tail of his shirt and pulled it off him, her hands ranging wild across his back, his chest, in his hair.

She tipped his head back to kiss him as he held the tops of her thighs against his hands. She gasped and reached out for the wall when one of his thumbs found her, hot and moist, between her legs. Her other hand gripped the railing till the knuckles turned white. He tortured her in a most pleasing manner.

When her knees could no longer hold her, he let her slide down his body to kneel before him, her arms gliding around his neck for support. He kissed her, hungry and possessive. She was sweeter than candy; more exciting than lightning. He wanted to crawl inside her skin and never leave her. She nipped and sucked at his breast, touched his hard arousal, and pulled at the tie string at his waist, her hands eager and untamed.

Pressing her back, he laid her beneath him on the blanket she'd stumbled over earlier. Surprised to feel it, she laughed softly.

"I'm sorry it's not a bed," he said, wishing he could give her silk sheets and scented feather pillows.

In the bright moonlight, she smiled at him.

"It's a wonderful bed," she whispered, kissing him softly. "The canopy is spectacular."

He could see the moon and the stars reflected in her eyes and knew full well that the rest of his universe lay beyond them, in her soul.

An emotion unlike any he'd known before filled him so completely, he thought he might rupture. It was a sensation greater than fear, richer than pride, beyond the tenderness of love—and she was the cause of it.

Unable to speak, he nodded, holding her face between his hands.

His expression scared her at first, until she recognized it as a need she knew too well; a need she dreamed about; a need that was basic and human and easily fulfilled. She reached out to him with arms as light as angel wings and pulled him to her, holding him close. She closed her eyes and smiled at the stars in her heart, at the world she held in her embrace, at the nightmare that faded from her mind, and the dream in her soul that she'd been so afraid would never come true.

He lifted his head to gaze at her in wonder, then he kissed her. Over and over. There and here. Between her breasts, below her ear. She spread her legs, eager to be filled. He laved her naval with his tongue and pressed gently on the trembling flesh of her thighs. He moved lower on her body until touching him was too great an effort for her pleasure-filled limbs. Licking and sucking, he pressured her to cry out.

Looming above her, feeling very like a victorious jungle beast, he waited for her to open her eyes and look at him. He felt her leg wrapping about his waist and watched her eyes, glazed and impetuous, as she impaled herself against him

Together they rocked the world off its axis.

NINE

It rained the next day, which was unusual for Arizona that time of year—though no one but the two of them suspected that it had anything to do with a recent planetary disruption.

In fact, they hardly noticed the rain. It was a bright sunny day in the lab. Kurt whistled as he worked. Mack hummed happily as she peered into the microscope.

"Oh! You're up, sleepyhead," Polly said from the doorway, acting surprised to see her. "I thought you were dead."

"Yes. I mean no. Yes, I'm up and no, I'm not dead," Mack said, shamefaced after sleeping till nearly noon, soundly and dreamlessly. "I can't believe I slept so late. Why didn't you wake me?"

"You think I don't hear you tossing and turning and prowling about at night? Not quite. You clearly needed your sleep, dear." Polly disappeared from the doorway, then returned a minute or two later. "Goodness gracious," she said, toting her books into the lab with a shake of her gray fuzzy head and a backward glance to the outer office. "I swear, it's like a sauna in there."

Mack frowned at her, confused. It was a perfect air-conditioned seventy-two degrees everywhere but in the greenhouse.

Polly fanned herself with her hand. "Very hot and humid. Very."

"Are you feeling all right?" Mack asked, concerned. "Come here and let me check you for a fever. Please, don't be sick. . . ."

"No, no, dear. Have no fear," Polly said. "I'm as healthy as a horse. Not as healthy as the two of them, of course"—she motioned with her head toward the office door—"but healthy enough to know when an old woman is impeding the course of true love. Heavens above."

Mack grinned. Joanne and Dwayne were in the outer office, and unless things had changed drastically since the night before, their exchange of steamy glances was, no doubt, fogging up the windows by now.

"Checking them for fevers and rashes could get a little tricky, don't you think?" Kurt asked, winking at Mack when she looked at him, feeling a little warm and itchy himself.

"Hide in here with us, Polly," she said, taking up Kurt's holier-than-"them" attitude, sure that as adults they were handling their emotions with far more discretion.

"Thank you, dear. There's nothing worse than feeling like an intruder."

Kurt left his stool to get something. As he passed behind Mack he dragged his hand across her backside affectionately. She very nearly followed after him like a love-starved puppy.

"Fiddle-dee-dee," Polly said, setting her books on

the worktable. "That reminds me . . . Eugene called and asked me to remind everyone that this building is equipped with outside surveillance cameras."

"What's that?" Mack asked, her eyes darting to Kurt while all the blood drained from her face. "Cameras?"

"Yes, dear, to watch the building from the outside," Polly explained kindly. "I suppose he was trying to ease our minds about burglars, but I can't for the life of me think why anyone would want to break into this place. Eugene is a strange fellow, don't you think? I'm just dying to meet him face-to-face."

Frankly, an encounter with Eugene was something Mack could do without, but even the thought of it wasn't enough to put an end to the silly grin that crossed her face—or to keep it from returning every time she looked at Kurt that afternoon.

Mack had no trouble keeping her CDC reports short and vague. No symptoms. No answers. Everyone was healthy and the A-B1 investigation was still under way. However, the distress in her expression when she hung up the phone that afternoon precluded a short vague response.

"What is it?" Kurt asked, watching her with concern.

She looked at him, shook her head, and smiled. "Nothing."

"Mack."

"Truly. Nothing's wrong."

A new sort of tension had wedged its way between them, and he wasn't going to tolerate it. Not this time. No secrets. Never again.

"Tell me."

For such a great actress, Mack was a really rotten liar.

Her smile fell away and she sighed. "Seventy-three more in Chad. Fifty-six in the Ukraine. A hundred and thirteen in the Yucatán. Two hundred and forty-two new cases in the past twenty-four hours. The numbers are decreasing, but . . ."

Mack didn't need to say more. The sadness and urgency in her voice was an equivalent to "Please find the answer soon." It was on the tip of her tongue to beg Kurt once again to let her help him, but she bit down hard and looked away. Making him angry would only slow things down.

"Mack," he said. "I'm sorry." He passed a frustrated hand through his hair. "I know what you're feeling. I do. I'm feeling it as well. But it just can't be A-B1. It can't be. Genetically, there's nothing to link it—"

"I know. I know," she said, wanting with all her heart to believe as he did. But the plain truth was, she didn't—yet. "They're still checking out other possibilities. Maybe one of those will pan out before . . . before long."

"I'd be the first to admit it if I thought for even half a second . . ."

"I know." She got up and walked over to him. "I know," she said again, her hand on his shoulder. She kissed him as an act of trust. "But we have to be absolutely sure."

For all of nature's infinite possibilities, it was amazing that science, the study of nature, was such a slow and ponderous occupation, with its strict methods and procedures and rigorously limited variables. No wonder that scientists themselves frequently fell into ruts. This being the case, it should have been predictable that after two nights of stealing away from the others, either Mack or Kurt would resist a change in venue.

"Someone will catch us. They're bound to start getting suspicious. You're not a very quiet lover and—"

"I'll be quieter, but I have to tell you, I don't care if we get caught or if we arouse suspicions. I want to be with you," he said, bullheaded, darling man that he was.

"I want to be with you too. And I don't really care who knows either, but it could get awkward."

"It's going to get awkward anyway, if you don't make up your mind. Do I come to you, or are you coming to me?" A pause. "Hell, I don't know why we're still waiting for everyone to fall asleep. We should kick 'em all off the couch at ten and go for it."

She clicked her tongue at him in disgust. "Leave it to me to fall in love with the last truly romantic man in—what?"

He was grinning at her. "You're in love with me?"

"Hardly. I fall into the arms of every handsome man I meet."

"You think I'm handsome?"

She closed her eyes. The man was impossible.

"As handsome as a truck-struck gofer, and almost as charming."

"Ow!" He clapped his hands to his bleeding heart. "How come you're not this mean when you're mad?"

"Because I'm too busy being mad to think straight."

"Well, we can't have any more of that," he said, leaning sideways to make sure they were alone in the greenhouse and that no one was in the lab, before taking her into his arms and pressing her back against the wall.

"Any more of what?" she asked, smiling with anticipation.

"Of you thinking straight," he said, then kissed her

silly. "That's better," he murmured a few minutes later. "I say we lock ourselves in my office for the duration of the quarantine. Then we find the biggest, softest bed in Arizona and make love till we die."

She giggled. "Can we eat first? I want real fried chicken and real grits and gravy and . . . and scrapple. Oh, scrapple. And a hamburger, a juicy one with lots and lots of grease and french fries that don't snap in half when you bend them, and—"

"Will you pay attention? I'm trying to get something going here, a little love in the afternoon for instance?"

"Oh, right. I forgot," she teased, her eyes shining. "What? I was joking," she added when he grew serious, his gaze intense and penetrating. "Kurt?"

He shook his head as he palmed her face. Seeing her happy, feeling the love that shimmered in her eyes, sensing his future in such a small frail package gave him one of those rare, overwhelming, thick-throated moments of perfect peace.

"You are so pretty," he said, smiling when she blushed and looked away. "I can't believe you don't know that."

Watching the front of his shirt rise and fall with his respiration, she shrugged and shook her head, firmly rooted in the state of disbelief.

Glancing up, she smiled. "I'm glad you think so."

He kissed her. "You're going to think so too," he promised her.

And if nothing else, he was a man of his word.

That night when she came to him, he undressed her in the moonlight. It was the simplest thing in the world to worship and adore her; to make her feel as if she were a goddess, bathed in silver stardust, wrapped in golden moonbeams, drenched in the scent of her own love.

"Why aren't you married?" Kurt pondered aloud, astounded she'd been alone so long, wondering if she'd ever been deeply in love before, if she'd ever felt anything close to what he was feeling. "Have you ever been in love?"

A long silence. They lay together in the fuzzy light of the night, their hearts at ease, their bodies satiated with lovemaking, unable to sleep, reluctant to forfeit one moment of their time alone.

"I've been in love. I think. But I don't live the kind of life that's conducive to marriage," Mack said. "Or raising children."

"So you don't think about marriage and children."

"I . . . think about them, I just don't have them." A sickening panic stirred in the pit of her stomach. She was positive that some marriages worked; she was sure that most children were wanted, but neither had been the case in her particular family experience.

"I was married once," he said, feeling she deserved to know.

"I know. Polly told me." Tipping her head upward on his chest, she could see enough of his face to know his expression was relaxed and carefree. "She called her a beast."

He chuckled, enjoying the description. "A jackal actually, though that particular image hadn't occurred to me until just now."

"Polly said she was the last lab partner you ever had."

"That's true," he said. "Remember, I told you that I spend more time in my lab than I do in my home?" She nodded. "When I was in graduate school, I met her in a lab. She was very beautiful and brainy and spent nearly as much time working as I did. She graduated about the same time I got the Kingsford Grant to test my thesis on a bifunctional bacteria."

"Andropov-B."

"I was on top of the world. I had the grant. I had the perfect friend, lover, and lab partner in one woman who was willing to marry me." A short ironic laugh. "I really thought I was cooking with gas in those days."

"What happened?"

After a short pause he said, "I mentioned brainy and beautiful, didn't I?" Mack nodded. She hoped he wouldn't mention it again. "Did I say anything about ambition?" Mack gave a single shake of her head. "She was very ambitious. And I won't tell you I didn't admire her for it; I did. I was ambitious myself. Extremely ambitious. We wanted the same things, I guess. We . . . just went after them from different directions."

"What was it you wanted?"

"What I still want. What we all want, I think. Recognition. Power and money, too, to be honest."

"And what did she want?"

"The same. Only she wanted the money first, then the power. Recognition would come with both."

"What happened?"

"The bifunctional bacteria would have brought me great recognition. Once I perfected it, I could have written my own ticket, worked on anything I wanted to. But it wouldn't have been—was never intended to be a fabulous moneymaker. And the fertilizer companies were scared to death that I'd do it. They'd be destroyed."

"But your first attempts failed, I remember. I suppose that made them feel better, for a while."

He nodded. "It should have, but then they had to

keep me from trying again. And with every failed attempt, the price was going up. . . ."

"The price?"

"They were paying a saboteur to make sure I failed."

She winced with imagined pain and shook her head. "Not your wife."

"Who else? And when the Kingsford Grant dried up and my budding reputation as a . . . brilliant young scientist was all but destroyed, they cut her loose; they didn't think they needed her anymore."

"Kurt, I'm so sorry."

He frowned. "You want to hear something weird? I hated her yesterday, have hated her for the past nine years. But telling that story to you just now, I . . . I feel sorry for her."

She could tell he was confused, wondering where all his malice and loathing had gone to suddenly. Even his posture changed; it relaxed, as if something had been drained out of him.

"She missed the boat, and you got back on and went on to fulfill your dream. I feel sorry for her too."

He smiled at her, aware for the first time—or perhaps simply remembering from long ago—that not all women are alike.

"What's your real name?" he asked out of the blue, thinking once again that her nickname was too tough and masculine for so feminine a female.

"If your first attempts to create a bifunctional bacteria were such a colossal failure, why did Agro-Chem give you a second chance?" she asked, ignoring his question.

"Dick Preston hired me for his department a few years later, after the dust settled. We worked together on a couple of projects."

"Biodegradable insecticides."

"Right," he said, flattered that she knew. "We became friends, and I told him how positive I was that a bifunctional bacterium was not only possible, but necessary to the environment. When he was promoted to president of Bio-Chem he gave me the go-ahead to work on it, in secret and in my spare time. And he made me vow it would be a bacterium specific to rice."

"Why?"

"He's the president of a fertilizer company. He was shooting himself in the foot, giving me a second chance to create a perpetual fertilizer, a onetime sale. But he was—is—also a scientist and a humanitarian, and he knows what fertilizers are doing to the environment. It was a moral dilemma for him."

She grinned. "But since sixty percent of the world lives on rice, and the richest farmers in the world grow wheat, he's willing to rob Peter to pay Paul. Charge wheat farmers more for their fertilizers to make up for what the company will lose with Andropov-B."

He nodded, but his smile was sad. "It's only a partial solution to the environmental problem, and it isn't going to hold Bio-Chem in the black for very long. If I can create A-B1 and make it specific to rice, someone else can do the same thing for wheat and corn."

"He's a brave man," she said, realizing that the strange Texan with the smoky voice whom she'd never met, only heard, would eventually lose his company altogether. Then something else occurred to her. "You're not thinking that A-B1 has been sabotaged again, are you? I mean, is that possible? Would someone risk killing all those people . . . ?" Her voice trailed away. It was entirely possible, and she knew it. "Oh no. How could they?"

"We don't know that they have yet. We don't even know yet if it's the bacteria that's killing them."

"And all this"—she waved her hand—"all this suspicion and secrecy and working alone and . . . all that's because you think someone, possibly even me, could be working for some fertilizer company that wants you to fail again?"

She wasn't insulted, only beginning to understand.

"Partly. If a man can't trust his wife, why would he trust a stranger?" That made sense. "But that isn't all of it, certainly not now. Mack, I know this bacterium inside out. I know how it works, how it thinks, how it reacts. I'm the only person in the world who'd recognize an anomaly in its behavior. If . . . if it's there, I want to be the one to find it."

She nodded and lowered her head back to his chest, understanding perfectly. It was his creation. Right or wrong, good or bad, he was responsible for it. The CDC could huff and puff and blow his house down, but it wouldn't change the end result. No matter what happened, the ultimate consequences—the miracle or the death of thousands of people—would come to rest on Kurt's shoulders alone.

With a renewed effort to be supportive and encouraging, with work to do, with her heart steeped in love, the days began to slip away.

Day five. Day six.

The best part of each day became the chance encounters with Kurt's gaze and watching as his mind traveled back to her and the love they shared. His features would relax. He'd smile at her affectionately. Then he'd wink and go back to work. Or, better yet, mosey across the room, steal a kiss, and then go back to work.

Day seven. Day eight.

"Are you catching a cold?" Kurt asked, after she'd blown her nose several times in the past few hours.

"Maybe," Mack said, tossing the tissue in the trash. "I don't really feel like it, but my nose is running like crazy today. It might be the air-conditioning. I can't remember the last time I spent this much time in it."

"Are you sure you're feeling well?" Polly asked, her brow furrowed with worry. "You know, you never can tell."

"Relax, Mother Hen. It's a little sniffle. My temperature was fine this morning and"—Mack put the back of her hand to her forehead—"I'm cool as a cucumber now."

Kurt cleared his throat, sounding annoyed at their chatter. It was something he did often, but seemed to be doing more and more now that he'd moved into the third phase of testing—the third generation of the Andropov-B bacteria, the third planting after the initial fertilization of the soil.

These were the grandchildren of Kurt's original bacteria, now very much at home in the soil and ready to attach themselves to the roots of a rice plant; to aid the plant in finding enough nutrients to thrive and grow. And as the fertilizer had been generally available for only the last three years, this was the crucial generation.

Kurt was anxious and tired, and if he was irritable, it was allowed. Even Mack was a little testy that day. Well, a lot really. The tension in her shoulders and neck was setting in like super-starch, making them stiff and scratchy.

By late afternoon of the eighth day of the quarantine,

the eleventh day of Kurt's investigation, the fifteenth day of mysterious deaths in three locations around the world, Mack had a headache that was threatening to blow the cap off of her skull.

Twice she'd taken an analgesic from the stash she kept with her toiletries for such occasions, but they hadn't yet kicked in. She was not one of those poor people prone to migraines, so the intensity of the pain concerned her—but then again, when was the last time she'd been under such acute pressure and stress? she told herself.

She pressed on her eyelids with her thumb and index finger, rubbing gently to ease some of the strain. It was becoming more and more difficult to focus, to concentrate, to think clearly. Both she and Kurt had been working hard, sleeping very little. She was exhausted. Her joints and muscles ached. A nap would cure everything.

It wasn't as if naps during the long, boring afternoons of their confinement were unprecedented. Polly took them routinely. Dwayne and Joanne had passed out once or twice from the tedium as well. A nap was definitely what she needed.

She turned, about to inform Kurt of her decision, and caught him with his eyes closed in defeat, his head resting against the eyepiece of his microscope.

In slow motion, like a boiling pot on a stove or a steaming volcano, he rose to his feet and exploded.

"Sonuvabitch!" He picked up the microscope and hurled it across the room, its electrical cord popping out of the socket. It dented a hole in the wall beside the door to the outer office. "Dammit to hell!" he said, pounding his fist on the countertop.

Shocked and frightened by the outburst, Mack said

nothing, knowing what was wrong. She could see it on his face. Feel it in the air around them.

Andropov-B had mutated spontaneously in the third generation. It was a killer.

"Good Godfrey! What's happening?" Polly shouted, entering the lab displaying a nap-induced "bed head."

"What's happening in here, man?" Dwayne ran into the room, turned around twice, then stopped to stare at the hole in the wall and the expensive instrument that had made it. "Wow. You okay, man?"

Kurt stared at each of them, but not at Mack. She watched as he took in deep breaths, one after another, in a valiant attempt to calm himself. Finally, he turned his head to look at her.

He was crushed.

"You'd better call your office," he said simply, softly. "We found the problem."

"No." It was as much a refusal to call as it was a denial of his conclusion. "Check it again."

"I already did."

"Then do it once more."

His disbelief took the form of an unnatural laugh. "What is the matter with you?" he asked. "This is what you wanted. This is what you came here for. You've got your answer. Call your office and tell them what's killing all those people—" He stopped short.

"Kurt. That's not fair. This isn't what I wanted. This—"

"All those people," he repeated without hearing her, crumbling like a castle built of sand. He staggered backward and caught himself on the stool. He sat down. "My God, all those people." He covered his face with his hands.

The pain in Mack's head was excruciating. It ran all

the way down her spine and into the backs of her legs. She rubbed at the itch on her neck. It was no minor effort to push her thoughts outward, away from herself and her own pain and disappointment.

"Kurt. Stop it," she snapped, too tired to be nice. "None of this is your fault. You know that. We don't have time for you to sit there feeling sorry for yourself."

Polly gasped at her cruel words. Dwayne frowned and looked as if he might attempt some sort of defense of his friend. Even Joanne was showing her disapproval. Only Kurt looked at Mack as if she might not be feeling quite herself at the moment . . . or, at the very least, had lost her mind completely.

She reached out and gripped the edge of the work counter, feeling sicker by the second, dizzy and nauseated.

"Please. Check it again," she said weakly. "Find out exactly when and why. It's important to know *why* it's happening, not just that it is. Don't tell anyone yet. It isn't going to make any difference now. Find out if and why it's isolated to those three locations. We can't condemn the whole project if the contamination is due to an outside influence. Please, Kurt. Don't give up."

She couldn't endure it any longer. Her hands rose up to hold the top of her head. Her back and legs hurt so bad, she could hardly stand. "I think I need an aspirin," she mumbled. "My head is . . . My whole body . . . Oh, gawd, I think I'm sick."

Kurt let out a sigh of exasperation as he rushed forward to take her in his arms before she fell over.

"Mack! Geez, why didn't you say something?"

"Don't yell at me."

"I'm not yelling."

"Then don't talk to me. Can't you *see* what's happening to my head?" She pushed at him in a feeble effort to maintain distance. "I don't feel good."

"I know, baby. Someone call somebody," he said to the others. He tossed her arms around his neck and let her hang on him. "She needs a doctor. She's on fire."

"I am?" She tried to lift her head to look at him, but it wasn't worth the pain, and now she was on fire too. "Kurt, I think I'm sick. I think I'm really, really sick. They're going to take me away. I'll be alone. Aw, gawd." She bent double as a cramp gripped her belly. "Bathroom," she muttered. "Quick."

He mostly dragged her into his office and then into the bathroom, hanging her over the toilet like a rag doll while she evacuated the contents of her stomach.

"Awk. Cafeteria food," she uttered when she could. "Go away, Kurt. I'll infect you. Please go."

"No way, bossy," he said, slapping a cool damp cloth to her face. "In case it's not uppermost in your mind right this second, let me remind you that you and I have shared a lot more than the same air for the past four or five days. If I'm going to catch anything from you, I've already got it."

"Oh," she cried miserably. "I'm so sorry. I'm sorry."

"Shhh." He pushed damp hair from her fevered brow and placed a kiss to her temple.

"We're gonna die," she said. "And it's all my fault."

"We're not going to die." He grunted a little, lifting her deadweight off the floor, maneuvering her feet-first out of the bathroom to the closest cot in his office.

"This one's Polly's."

He didn't care, but what he said was, "Polly won't care."

"I bet I've contaminated her too. Good golly, poor sweet Polly. Trolley. Dolly. Miss Molly," she said as her body flopped onto the cot. She felt like a bag of flour splitting wide open, though Kurt was handling her as gently as he might liquid hydrogen. "I wish . . ."

"What? What do you wish?" he asked, slipping the cloth tie at her waist and pulling the scrub bottoms off her from below.

"I wish Polly . . . ugh . . . I wish . . . What are you doing?"

"I can see where you might wonder. I've actually done this more gracefully, I know, but I'm trying to undress you. You have a fever. I'm going to cool you off, give you a sponge bath, pack you in ice if I have to."

"Well, some of that sounds okay," she said, really wishing he'd just leave her alone. "But I'd rather not be packed in ice, thank you."

"You might not have a choice. I . . . Aw, geez, Mack."

"What now?"

"Petechia. You're covered with them."

She tried to lift her head off the pillow to look at the rash of tiny blood-filled blisters scattered over her body, and whimpered at the pain of the exertion. There was a red-hot poker stuck in her neck, and she couldn't bend it.

"I don't care," she said, apathetic. "Why don't we leave the rest and sleep for a while. Okay?"

"Soon. I'm going to sit you up for a second, to get this top off." He was huffing and puffing at the task, despite Joanne's stepping in to help hold up Mack's torso.

"No, no, no. It hurts. Leave it. Go away. Go, Joanne, you'll get sick. Make her go away. Ow, ow, ow. Stop it. Dammit, Kurt. It hurts. Don't you understand?"

"I understand. Thanks, Joanne. I think she may be right about you hanging around. No sense in all of us getting sick. I can handle her." He looked down into fever-bright green eyes as he covered her near-naked body, flushed and splotched, with the bedsheet. "Right? I can handle you, can't I?"

"In your dreams, pal."

He chuckled at that. It was such a nice sound.

"I wish," he said under his breath, hoping against hope that he'd wake up soon. "Have you taken anything for the pain?"

She said she had, then closed her eyes and tried to ignore him. He went back to the bathroom, wet two large bath towels with cold water, and tried to drape them across her body from her shoulders to her knees and from her knees down. She threw and kicked them off as fast as he could spread them.

"Mack. Stop it."

"You stop it."

"You're going to fry your brain if you don't leave these alone."

"They're cold," she said, though she did stop fighting him. "Go back to work, Kurt. I'll just take a little nap here."

He went back to the bathroom for two more wet towels. She was heating them up almost as quickly as he put them on her.

"Kurt! Kurt," she cried, sitting up, suddenly agitated, the wet towels falling away from her body.

"What?" he said, taking up her urgency as he sat down beside her, making an effort to push her back onto the cot. But she grabbed his shirtfront and shook him till his head rattled.

"You have to call my mother," she said. "It won't be pleasant for you, I know, but someone has to do it and . . . and I'm not really up to it."

"Okay. Sure. Lie down and tell me what you want me to tell her."

She clicked her dried-out tongue at him. "Tell her I'm *sick*."

He chuckled at her expression. He couldn't help it. If he didn't make light of the situation, it would pulverize him to a weeping heap of uselessness. "Anything else?"

"Yes," she said, fading fast. Her burst of energy depleted, she lay back on the cot and closed her eyes, rolled on her side to face the wall, and drew her legs up to her chest.

"Mack?" His panic eased when she groaned in response. He started draping the towels again. "What else would you like me to tell your mother?"

He waited, watching her breathe in and out, and finally decided that she'd dozed off. Tears pressed against the backs of his eyes until it hurt, and he closed them. He wasn't a particularly religious man, but his chosen profession and common logic demanded that he believe in a higher power. Something or someone with more control over nature than man would ever have or could ever dream of having. And it was to this power that he prayed for Mack's life . . . for his life.

TEN

Mack was conscious but not really awake. If she lay very still, it didn't hurt too bad. And if she kept her eyes closed, no one disturbed her. They stopped talking to her—talked *about* her instead.

"Where the hell is the doctor?" Kurt sounded so worried, but there wasn't a thing she could do about it—or felt like doing about it.

"He's coming, dear. How is she?"

"Not good. Too hot. Stiff. Horrible pain. The petechia . . . It looks like meningitis. It was Neisseria, right? Meningococcal?"

"I'm afraid so." Kurt cursed. "Of course, you've considered that it could be any one of them or even more than one."

Mack didn't listen to any further speculations. She was busy trying to recall the chapters on meningococcal meningitis in her pathology books. Acute inflammation of the pia mater, the delicate tissue that covers the brain and spinal cord, sometimes the membrane lining the cerebral ventricles too. That certainly explained the pain.

She envisioned pools of pus in her brain stem. She'd slip into a coma, and the toxins would get her before the pain killed her.

A small comfort, at this point.

"If they try to take her out of here, I'm going with her," she heard Kurt say. "Will you handle things for me here? Call the Centers for Disease Control, tell them about the bacteria, they can do whatever they feel is necessary with it. And . . . well, I'll call my mom. I need her mother's number. Can you find it for me?"

There was a short silence during which she debated arguing with him about his plans. He should stay and find out why A-B1 was mutating. The more he was exposed to her, the higher the risk to his own health. He shouldn't worry his mother until he was symptomatic. Her mother . . .

"Tell her . . ."

"What? Say it again, Mack."

She tried to wet her lips, but her tongue was like sandpaper. "Don't yell."

"I'm not," he whispered close to her ear, barely breathing. "Go on."

"My mother. Tell her . . . I'm sorry."

"You're sorry?"

She knew she'd die for sure if she tried to nod her head.

"I'm sorry about Papa," she mumbled. She rested a second or two. "I'm sorry that if . . . if she had to have a baby . . . I'm sorry I wasn't . . . I wasn't the daughter she wanted."

"I'm not going to tell her that," he said flat out. "I'm going to tell her to catch the next plane to Phoenix and—"

She started to cry. The man was truly impossible.

"Mack. You're going to be fine. I promise," he said, trying to convince the both of them as he wiped a tear from the tip of her nose with his thumb. "They'll pump you full of penicillin and you'll be fine in a few days."

"I don't want to die," she whimpered. The pain in her head was back without warning, a screaming pain, consuming her, tearing her apart, eating her alive.

"You are absolutely not going to die. I forbid it. Do you hear me? By the time your mother gets here, your fever will be—"

"I'm a mess. She'll be angry." She had to hold on to something. She was drowning in the pain.

"Mack, honey, you're delirious. Your mother'll be worried, but she won't be angry. She'll want to be with you."

She couldn't stand it. She swung her arm twice to hit him in the neck, and twice more to get his arm.

"You're such a spoiled brat," she screamed at him, sitting up, shredding what was left of her brain. "Don't you understand anything? I was an accident. I wasn't supposed to happen. My papa was poor white trash. I'm the worst thing that ever happened to her. She never wanted me, and nothing I ever did was good enough to change her mind. She's not your mother, you know. She's mine. I think I ought to know how she's going to react."

"Okay. I'm sorry. You're right. Lie back. You're right. I'll . . . I'll tell her you're sorry."

"Okay." Too weary and dizzy to say or do more, she returned to her fetal position to ease the strain on her muscles. "Thank you," she added, recalling her manners.

Mack was grateful for any unconscious respite that came along, as they seemed to off and on. However, if she was aware of those around her, she wasn't letting on. She didn't have the energy.

She assumed a doctor finally arrived from somewhere, but she didn't catch his name or anything he had to say. She could vaguely recall Kurt's comforting voice and a heavy pressure low in her back and some discussion about milky spinal fluid, but that was about all. That and a feeling they were drugging her with a pain medication.

"Take a deep breath, Mack," Kurt would whisper in her ear persistently until she obeyed. "That's my girl."

She had no concept of time either. Chance inspections told her she was either going blind or they'd darkened the room . . . or she was having the longest nightmare ever recorded.

There were hands, but they weren't mean or hurtful. They made her cold and soothed her in turn. They were nice hands, friendly, loving.

Once she accidentally opened her eyes and thought she saw Kurt sleeping on a cot beside her. There was an intravenous catheter in her forearm, her lips were bumpy, and her mouth felt like a desert. She closed her eyes again, apathetic.

"Why don't you go somewhere? Do something. You're making me crazy," she said, clearly and abruptly in the middle of the second night of her raging fever. "What's this?" She picked at the plastic beneath the sheet.

"It's a cooling blanket. Leave it alone," Kurt told her, waking immediately but not getting up. She talked constantly, mumbled more often then not, but nothing she said or mumbled made any sense.

"Did you find out why . . . the bugs went nuts."

Bugs was shorter and easier to say and remember than bacteria and all the names he had for it.

"What bugs? Mack? Do you know where you are?" he asked, getting up on one elbow, his hopes wedged in his throat.

"I won't tolerate being beaten like this. When I'm better, I'm leaving you."

A half laugh, half gasp of frustration escaped him. "Okay. I think you should. Are you hurting pretty bad?"

"How would you feel if a truck ran over you?" she wanted to know.

"Pretty bad, I guess. Want some water?"

"Good idea."

"Thanks," he said, getting up slowly. Sitting on the side of his cot in his skivvies, he reached for the water and lifted her up from the middle of her back to drink from the straw. He was probably imagining it, but she seemed a little more flexible. "How's that? Good?"

"Mmmm," she agreed, looking at him with remarkable clarity in her eyes. "I can't remember," she said, distressed. "Did we ever have children?"

He closed his eyes to hide his disappointment, then opened them and smiled at her. "We have six beautiful, healthy, happy children who are all wishing you'll get well soon."

A small wistful, contented smile crossed her lips, and she let him lay her back down. "Six. Imagine that."

"Yeah, imagine that." He brushed the hair from her forehead with the cool palm of his hand, then bent and kissed her there. "Imagine that, and have sweet dreams."

"Okay."

The past two days were the longest he'd ever known. Both the nurse, who'd moved in with them, and the doctor, who came by three or four times each day, kept telling him that Mack's confusion was normal, but for so long? What about permanent brain damage? He rubbed the back of his aching neck, staring at his bare feet.

He'd made so many promises. *Get well and I promise you won't be sorry. I'll love you forever, just please don't leave me.*

He supposed he should have been surprised that she'd become so much a part of him in so short a time, but he wasn't. He had a feeling he loved her before he ever met her; obsessed about her during puberty; dreamed about her in his youth; looked for her everywhere. She was everything he'd ever fantasized about.

Please, let her live and I'll never lose my temper again. I'll never be too proud or stubborn or jealous or think evil thoughts about anyone, or . . . or take her for granted or argue with her or . . . or anything else. Please. Let her live.

"Pssst." She was watching him. Eyes clear and searching. He smiled at her. "Did you blab our secret to anyone?"

He lifted his eyebrows in question. "Which secret is that? We have several."

She wiggled her finger at him, he moved closer, and she whispered, "The one about the bugs."

He reached out and held her finger, played with the short little nail. "Don't worry about the bugs anymore, Mack. That's all taken care of. No one else is going to die."

"Then you know why?"

"Why what, baby?"

"Why they went bad?"

He no longer cared. He would accept his failure with Andropov-B if only she would get well.

"It doesn't matter why. We know now, and we won't let them hurt anyone else."

She frowned. "You don't know why?" She seemed confused inside her confusion. "I want to know why. You have to find out why." She started picking at the sheet again, her eyes darting wildly, her agitation mounting. "You said you'd find out why. I need to know why. I want an answer. Go get me an answer, Kurt. Go get it now."

"Okay, okay. Relax." He wasn't sure which he hated seeing more, Mack dull and listless or Mack disturbed and delirious. "It doesn't matter anymore why it happened."

"It matters to me. I want to know why."

"Okay. I'll find out for you." Their voices had roused the nurse, who had been sleeping on the third cot behind Kurt, and she'd come to stand behind him.

"Now."

"Mack, honey, it's the middle of the night. First thing in the morning—"

"Now!"

"Mack . . ."

"Now! Now! Now!" she said, coming up off the bed, taking several wide swings at him.

"Okay," he shouted back at her. "Knock it off. Lie down and I'll leave. I'll start looking for your answer." He was striking a deal with a crazy woman, he knew, but to tell the truth it beat sitting around watching her slowly dying.

"Promise me."

"I promise."

Because of the thermal blanket and the cool damp towels they were using to control her temperature, the soaking perspiration when her fever broke went unnoticed.

In her dreams, she and Kurt were camping at the beach. She was wet and cold . . . and she ached all over.

"Tide's coming in," she said to whoever was squeezing her arm. "My sleeping bag's wet."

"Dr. McKissack? Can you hear me?" asked an unfamiliar voice. "You're soaking wet, but you're not in a sleeping bag."

"Did I fall off a cliff?"

"No, ma'am. You've been ill." The pressure around her arm slowly eased away. "But you're going to be just fine. Your fever broke. Dr. Andropov? Dr. Andropov, she's awake."

"Kurt?" Mack reached out behind her to feel for his sleeping bag. "Kurt?"

"I'm here," he said, taking her hand. "Mack?"

"Hmmm?" She rolled onto her back and was immediately sorry. "Aww, ow."

"It's all right. You don't have to move. Just open your eyes and talk sense to me."

She frowned. "Cents? Like money?"

"Close enough, now open your eyes."

She did. He studied them, then smiled at her. She smiled back.

"Hi," he said. "How do you feel?"

She took a moment to think about it. "Okay. How do you feel?"

"Terrific. How's your head? Do you hurt?"

"Yes. All over. What happened?" She closed her eyes. "I've been sick." Her next thought pained her, and she opened her eyes. "The others . . . are they . . . ?"

"We're all fine. We're all taking more penicillin, enough to grow mold in our ears—except for Dwayne. He's allergic. They have him on tetracycline. But we're all fine. Worried about you, but fine."

"She says I'm going to be fine too." Mack indicated the nurse.

"That's Lucy, our nurse." Mack nodded, then winced with the pain. "We also get visits from a doctor now. Dick has spared no expense."

"How long?"

"This is the third day. When you're better, we're going to beat the crap out of you for extending the quarantine," he said, grinning at her. "The day you got sick, we went back to day one."

"Sorry," she said, tired again. "But thanks for waiting till I feel better."

"Don't believe him for a second," Polly said, standing in the doorway. When Mack tried to look at her, she moved into the room to make it easier. Dwayne and Joanne squeezed in too. "We're so happy you're better, we're planning another party. Dwayne says we should party hearty with real beer and country music this time."

Dwayne was starting to rhyme too?

"Man, I said we should rock the night away. Doc suggested the country stuff."

Amused, Mack smiled weakly. She would have chuckled, but her ribs hurt. She felt tears in her eyes and had an overwhelming sensation of feeling grateful. She wasn't going to die. She had people who loved her. Life was a perfect, precious gift.

Sleep, no longer an escape but a short period of rejuvenation, was still uncontrollable and sporadic. She was aware of falling asleep and waking up in the middle of different conversations. She'd doze off smelling breakfast eggs and bacon and come around to the sounds of David Letterman on the television in the next room.

The pain in her joints and muscles ebbed to a dull

ache that came in waves whether she was moving or not. She was weak and had to concentrate to control her limbs.

Once she came awake sitting straight up on Kurt's lap, his arms supporting her. She tipped her head back to look at him.

"This is the best part of my day," he told her, smiling down into her face. "I get to hold you like this while Lucy makes your bed." He studied her for a moment or two. "I'd kiss you, but you've got gunk on your mouth for the fever blisters." He pressed a sweet one to her brow instead. "Are you comfortable? Am I hurting you?"

With hardly any effort at all, she looped her free arm around his neck and held him tight. "You are the nicest spoiled brat I've ever known."

His chest bounced when he chuckled, spreading a happy warm feeling through her. She sighed and decided to spend the rest of her glorious life right where she was.

"Where is everyone?" she asked after a while.

"Watching TV in the other room."

"How are they?"

"Good. We composed a Dear Myrna letter yesterday. Dwayne didn't think it was fair to leave her hanging, now that he and Joanne are sleeping in the greenhouse together. And he didn't feel he could tell her over the phone, because she'd yell at him, or maybe cry, he said."

"They're sleeping together?"

"Well, she can't sleep in here, and there's been an empty cot in there since the beginning, and Polly spends most of her day on my couch anyway, and I've been staying in here . . . so we played a little musical beds, and they took the greenhouse."

It was too strange a picture. . . .

"How's it going?" she asked after another little while,

during which she may have fallen asleep. It was hard to tell sometimes.

"Good now," he said. "The doctor says you'll be weak for a while longer but—"

"No," she said, stopping him. "With A-B1. How's it going? Do you know what happened yet?" She looked at him when he didn't answer right away. He wouldn't look back at her. "Kurt?"

"No," he said, short and reluctant. "I don't know any more now than I did when you first got sick, except that it is isolated." Her expression, when he finally glanced at her, was an invitation to explain further. "At least it appears to be isolated . . . for now. The Ukraine, Chad, the Yucatán. They're the only soil samples where the mutated organism shows up so far . . . and only . . . well, I started a fourth generation to see if it's only a matter of time before it mutates everywhere."

"And only what?" she asked, noting his hesitation.

He smiled, loving the idea that she was alert enough now to pick up on verbal nuances. Of course, in a few weeks he'd probably be feeling differently about it, but . . .

"It probably doesn't mean anything, but the anomaly doesn't appear in all the samples from the same country." What did that mean? she speculated, trying to focus her thoughts. "I have soil samples from two sites in the Yucatán, four in Chad, and five from the Ukraine. The pathogen appears in only one sample from each country, two in the Ukraine." He shrugged. "I'm guessing that given more time, it'll show up in all the samples."

Lucy had finished with the bed and wanted Mack back in it, so it was some time before she could ask, "Why are you assuming it'll show up in all the samples?"

He was startled to be back on the same subject. He shrugged. "I don't know." He laughed softly. "I'm not even too sure why I'm pursuing it at all, except that you had such a hissy fit about it the other night, and I had nothing better to do."

"You're wrong," she said. "It's not a matter of time. It can't be. It has to be some outside influence. Contaminated soil . . ."

"Nope. I checked. Plain old dirt." He didn't like the look on her face. That mulish, half-crazed, more than a little confused expression she'd taken on in her delirium. "But I don't want you lying in here worrying about this. I told you I'd find an answer for you and I will. You worry about getting stronger." He leaned over to murmur in her ear, "I need you."

She was almost as pleased as she was embarrassed. She was fairly certain she looked like an expression of a mad artist's hell. It was difficult to believe that he was still seeing her as desirable.

"She blushes and it's not a fever," he said, teasing her, though it sounded more as if it were a prayer of thanks.

"I never blush," she said, feeling warmer around the ears.

"The hell you don't," he said, kissing her cheek. "Now go to sleep. We'll talk more later."

"Okay, but don't assume it's time. Okay?"

"Okay."

Mack gathered it was for ventilation purposes, and guessed that the nurse, Lucy, was bored sick of watching her sleep, that the two doors to Kurt's office were now being left open while she dozed off and on during the day. For whatever reason, she was glad of it. She wasn't up to entertaining the troops yet, but it was a comfort to listen to them going on with their lives.

With the head of her cot just inside the door to the lab, she knew Kurt and Polly spent most of their time together in the lab working, and that in the outer office Dwayne, Joanne, and Lucy were losing to the real contestants on the television game shows they tuned in to.

Her eyes would blink open. She'd find another more comfortable position on the cot, listen to the familiar voices for a while, and fall back to sleep. Whole days must have passed that way, though she had no idea how many.

It was very strange. Like a limbo of sorts. She was better, but not well. Conscious, but not thinking. Happy, but not enthusiastic. Her thoughts were scattered pieces of memory, fact, and dreams.

"You know, this reminds me of something," she heard Polly saying when next she woke. "It's ringing a bell in my head. Ding. Ding. But I'm not sure why."

In a half sleep, she listened to see whom she was talking to, but no response came, and Polly went on.

"Look here, when it first begins, look at the cell walls. What is that? They look blistered. Like they've been burned, don't they?"

"Yeah, I guess," Kurt said, distracted. "A little."

"Then here, on this slide, whatever that is permeates the cell wall and is absorbed into the bacteria."

"It looks that way, I know, but it doesn't have the same molecular structure. The stuff inside the cells is a protein derivative. It might even be part of the cell wall itself, changed by whatever is attacking it from the outside. Question is, what's attacking it in the first place."

"Animal? Vegetable? Mineral? That's the name of the game."

Good. Kurt hadn't given up on Andropov-B, and Polly was helping him. Old dogs *could* learn new tricks.

She went back to sleep.

ELEVEN

"Okay, deadhead, rise and shine," Kurt said, whipping the covers off her.

She pushed at the hospital gown, imported specially for her use, trying to cover herself up again.

"Go away. I'm sleeping," she said, keeping her back to him. She'd ignored him the first two times he'd called her. He wasn't much for taking a hint, was he?

"Not anymore you're not," he said. "The doctor says you can have a bath today, and Lucy and I concur that you definitely need one."

If that was his way of saying "You stink" he wasn't being very nice. She was an invalid, after all.

"I had a bath yesterday," she said.

"A sponge bath. You haven't had a real bath in five days."

"Go away. Lucy can bathe me later."

"It's the shower for you," he said, and then overcome with a touch of Pollyitis, he added, "boo-boo."

"Don't be stupid. I can't take a shower. I can hardly stand up."

"I know. That's why I'm taking it with you."

She rolled onto her back then, and looked at him. He wagged his brows at her as if he were a dirty old man.

"*With* me?"

He nodded, looking cheeky. "I volunteered."

"No." She folded her arms across her chest for emphasis.

"Oh, yes," he said, leaning over to pull her into a sitting position. "I've got some good news for you, and I want you to be wide-awake when you hear it."

"I am awake, thank you. Take your hands off me."

"Ha. That's a far cry from the tune you were singing a week ago, Doctor." He pulled her midsection up to a level with his, and the rest of her body followed.

"That was a week ago. We can discuss this again a week from tomorrow, how's that?"

"Pretty good, but it isn't going to work. Come on. That's it," he said, waiting for her legs to stop wobbling. "All your tubes are out, you're eating and drinking, and now a shower. You're almost as good as new. Come on. You're going to love this. I'm good at this."

"Huh," she huffed. She just bet he was.

"You're mean and nasty too. These are all excellent signs of your recovery."

He held her upper arms to lend balance and walked backward. She couldn't do anything but follow with stilted steps and an angry frown.

"All right, all right. But I'm going alone. What's everyone going to say when they find out we're taking showers together?"

"Hmmm. That's a tough one," he said. "Dwayne'll probably congratulate me, and the girls'll say . . . they wish it was them," he concluded, for lack of a better answer.

"I'm serious."

"So am I. About you. And everyone knows it. This isn't going to shock anyone."

Ah, hell. Why did she care anyway? It wasn't as if she had any dignity left. Stripped naked. Delirious. Poked. Prodded. She sighed. Life was too short to worry about what other people were thinking. It was too short to give a man all the love he deserved; all the love she had to give him. And it was way too short to fight about taking a shower.

"Sorry," she said as he eased her down on the lid of the commode. "You've been really great to me during all this."

"Yes, I have." He reached into the shower to turn the water on, then pulled his shirt off over his head.

"I've been wanting to say thank you, but mostly I just snap at you. I'm sorry."

"I forgive you," he said, letting his pants drop to the floor, standing before her, tall, naked, and beautiful. "Stand up."

She tried pushing off the commode, but her heart was free-floating in her chest, up in her throat, down to her stomach, beating too fast; her nerve endings were in spasm. She was flustered, excited, nervous, and too weak to do anything about anything. She needed his arm and a lift to get up. He reached behind her to untie her gown. It fell off, landing on the floor between them.

Right away he knew this was going to be the ultimate test of his machismo. He started to swell like a hot-air balloon. She stood before him, eyes downcast, with no idea of how sweet and vulnerable she looked; without an inkling of how beautiful her body was to him; unable to imagine how much he wanted her at that moment. He recalled what a miracle it was that she was alive; in his life, in his soul. He recalled all the promises he'd made, his dreams about their future together.

Slowly her gaze lifted from the floor to meet his, humor lurking behind the regret and apprehension. He shrugged and gave her a what's-a-man-to-do? grimace.

"Sorry," she said, grinning, tense and unskilled in this sort of situation, trying not to laugh.

"It's all right." He grinned back at her, playfully kissing the tip of her nose. "It happens every time you cross my mind."

Laughing together, he led the way to the shower, where a stool had been set under the falling water. Two adult bodies, plus furniture, in the already small shower led to some very tight quarters.

"Take the stool out," she said at the door. "You're all I'll need." He smiled as if she'd flattered him and removed the stool.

For the first second only did it feel as if she were being peppered with buckshot, then the water softened to warm fat drops of tranquilizing bliss, streaming down her body, loosening taut muscles, washing away the past five days of pain.

"Oh," was all she could utter as her body went limp with the pleasure and she sagged against him. He held her against him, washing her as he ran his hands up and down her body. Gently massaging aching muscles. Soothing with warmth. Reaffirming over and over in his mind that she was there, with him, alive and well.

"Oh," she muttered again, her hair full of suds, his fingers on her scalp.

"Didn't I tell you you'd love this?" he asked, his affection for her keeping his hands gentle and undemanding. She made a purring noise against his chest. "Didn't I tell you everything would be fine?" he said, his voice catching on the lump of emotion in his throat.

She lifted her head to look at him. The toll of the past five days was etched all over his face. His pain was as sharp as any she'd known.

"I . . . With all that's been going on, I bet I forgot to tell you how much I love you," she said, touching the gray hair at his temple, imagining she saw a few more now. He nodded, saying nothing, but letting her know that he wouldn't mind hearing it again. "I love you."

Good intentions gone up in steam, he bent his head to kiss her. Her slick wet body slid up to meet him.

"Mack . . ." His voice was cautionary when her lips moved to his ear and she started to nibble at his neck. She took the nubby nipple of his breast into her mouth, and he trembled, tried to push her away. "Mack . . ."

Granted, no love dance was going to be performed in the shower that day, but she knew a few ways of expressing her love and appreciation. And mere mortal that he was, he didn't put up much resistance to accepting her gifts. Rather, he held her when she was finished, close to his pounding heart, closed his eyes, and thanked whomever it was that had answered his prayers.

When he regained the strength to be of assistance, he helped her out of the shower and dried her off. But instead of taking her back to the cot, he suggested she sit in a chair while he combed out her hair.

"I can do it, I think." She reached for the brush on the table beside her cot. "I'm actually feeling sort of . . . perky after my shower. What about you?"

He pulled his shirt down into place then leaned forward to examine the front of his pants. "Perky? Nnnnot anymore, I'm afraid. But better. That shower definitely made a new man of me."

They laughed as lovers will, and he took the brush from her. "Let me do it this time. I need to tell you something."

"That's right," she said, recalling what he'd said before. "You said it was good news."

"It is. I'm just not sure how you'll take it."

She looked at him expectantly. "You've found out why A-B1 is mutating."

"No."

"But you're close."

"Not even."

"Then what's your good news?"

"Your mother's here."

Silence.

"I called when you first got sick. Like you asked," he said, speaking quickly. "She wasn't home. The housekeeper said she was away on a trip and that she'd relay my message as soon as she heard from her." The last time they spoke, her mother had mentioned a trip, but Mack hadn't paid any attention to the dates. "Anyway, I guess the message got relayed, because now she's here. In Phoenix."

Not a word or even a resigned sigh.

"She's worried about you." When she didn't respond, he asked, "So? What do you think?"

"I think I'm ready to go back to bed."

"Mack. She wants to talk to you. As soon as you're well enough, she said."

"Oh, dear." Nothing inside her could make her wish for a relapse just to avoid talking to her mother. "I suppose I could call her on the phone, as long as I don't have to see her," she said, thinking aloud. "That shower wasn't that great. And I still have, what? Another nine or ten days to pull myself together?"

He frowned with concern. "She's not going to care what you look like. She just wants to know you're okay. You don't even have to talk to her today, if you don't want to." She glanced at him. "She sent this up this morning."

He pulled a letter from the back pocket of his scrubs and handed it to her. She turned it over in her hands, recognized the writing on the front, then lowered it to her lap.

"Aren't you going to read it?"

"Later. I'm a little tired. I think—"

"Mack," he said gently, squatting down beside her. "Will you let me read it to you?" She questioned his insistence. "I've talked to her on the phone."

"She's very polite, isn't she?"

"Yes. Very. And very concerned about you. I think you should read the letter. Or let me read it to you."

She wanted to ask why. Why did he care when she didn't? The letter would be a list of precautions to be taken during her recovery, a reminder that her mother had never approved of her job, and if she was lucky a few juicy tidbits of Vicksburg gossip, to keep her on top of things at home. *Why* did she have to read it now?

"You can read it, if you want," she said, handing it back to him, squelching the urge to ask him to do so in silence.

"Good girl." He praised her as if she were making a great sacrifice.

He was dying to read the letter. It was hard to imagine the relationship—or rather nonrelationship—Mack had with her mother, given his own parent's huge influence in his life. The polite conversation he had with her on the phone had shed little light on the woman; perhaps the letter would help him to understand this creature who Mack believed couldn't love her.

He sat on the floor at her feet, opened the letter, and started reading it from her lap.

" 'My dear Penny,' " he began. He looked up. "Penny?" She sighed laboriously. "It's Penny? Like . . . Penelope?"

"No. It's just plain Penny," she said, hating the name more than she ever had before. "I once heard her tell someone that she offered my father a penny for his thoughts one night, and he'd taken her literally. I didn't get it at first, but eventually I figured out what he'd had on his mind that night, and that I was the penny she gave him."

He could tell she still didn't appreciate the story. But he did.

"It's not funny."

"A penny for your thoughts? Are you kidding? Considering her predicament at the time, I think your mother must have maintained a wonderful sense of humor about the whole thing."

"You're a sick man. Stop laughing. If you think that's humor, you and my mother are going to get along real well." She waited. "Are you going to read that or not?"

"Yes." He cleared his throat. "Where was I?"

"Dear Penny."

"Oh yeah," he said, then he corrected her. "*My* dear Penny."

"Despair gives courage to the weak"—Somerville. It seems so when one has nothing left to lose. It's a shame really. And yet I find it to be an absolute truth at this moment.

I know that you and I have found it difficult

over the years to agree on any topic generally considered to be within the realm of polite conversation, but it has occurred to me—perhaps too late—that we might have found a plane of greater understanding if we had spoken to each other on a more personal level.

For instance, despite the fact that I have frequently cautioned you on the follies of being prideful, are you aware of how proud I am of you? And while I have tried to temper your spontaneity, your willful disregard for convention, and your determination to live your own life, with a sense of prudence, deliberation, and a certain amount of healthy trepidation, can you try to imagine how much I have admired your spirit? Would it surprise or amuse you to know that I have frequently—most often in the heat of our stormy disputes, I think—wished to be more like you?

How different our lives might have been if I'd had your strength of faith in your convictions. What if I had your determination to succeed on your own merits? Where would we be now if I'd had your courage to love?

This is not the first time I have asked these questions.

It has been to your own advantage, I believe, that you were never a vulnerable, helpless child who needed a great deal of mothering. I would have failed you miserably in that respect as well, I fear, for I am not a demonstrative woman by nature. The few times I have allowed my emotions to carry me away have not turned out well, to say the least. I offer you no explanations or excuses for who I am or what I've done with my life except to ask that you keep in mind one basic fact.

My regrets are few.

I was, and still am, I suppose, hopelessly in love with your father. He was the most handsome, self-confident, intelligent, amusing man I have ever met or ever hope to meet. You are my heart and soul. I regret only that I was unable to demonstrate my love to those who wanted it most, and that now when you might possibly feel a need for me, I am unable to be with you.

Your friend Dr. Andropov tells me that, barring any complications, you have weathered the worst of your illness, and once again I am too late, with too little to offer you. Please accept my sincerest wishes for a speedy recovery and any comfort you might take in knowing that my thoughts are with you.

"Did she sign it?" she asked after a long period of silence.

"Yes," he said, looking back to the letter. " 'In hope, Mother.' "

A lopsided smile. "She hates it when I call her mother. Not the word, but the way I say it. It sort of defines the formality in our relationship. It reminds her that there's a conspicuous abnormality between us, and if she can feel it, so can everyone else."

He heard it. She made the endearment sound like a synonym for cold rock.

"She writes a nice note, doesn't she?" she asked, closing her eyes, looking tired. He thought it was the saddest thing he'd ever read. "I believe that's the first one she's ever signed," she went on, as if this puzzled her. "I used to get a ton of them from strangers . . . like 'Vice stings us even in our pleasure, but virtue consoles us even in our pains—Colton' when I lost my virginity. And 'Life is a long lesson in humility—James M. Barrie' when I told her I was going to college to make something of my life and that I didn't need her money or permission to do it. Even Oscar Wilde wrote to me once: 'The Book of Life begins with a man and a woman in a garden. It ends with Revelations.' It was the anonymous notes that I always suspected were from her. 'The one splash of color in your closet is a new dress for the Andersons' garden party. Please wear it.' And 'I wish to speak with you at your earliest convenience. Please leave your attitude behind' was always one of my favorites. But she never signed them. I guess she just assumed I knew her handwriting."

He was glad her eyes were closed; it was tough enough not to laugh, but he couldn't stop the grin on his face. She was describing a classic mother-daughter love-hate relationship. Two women so much in love with each other and so much alike that all they ever seemed to do was reach out in need and then hurt each other.

A little effort, a little understanding, and he could see there was hope for both of them. Her mother was making the effort, and it was well within Mack's capabilities to provide the understanding, given the time.

TWELVE

Being an invalid was humiliating, at best. Mack was completely dependent on the whims of others. Namely Kurt. Harboring an affection for a man who had not the slightest regard for her own wishes was becoming difficult as he plopped her down in front of the television in the outer office among her fellow captives. She needed to socialize a little, he said. She needed to gain her strength back, he insisted. She needed to take an interest in the world again, he decided unilaterally.

She suffered well-meant comments on her much-improved appearance—that of a zombie with a dead battery or perhaps the winner in a rigor mortis competition. Then, between covert, anxious glances in her direction, they all pretended not to have a near-death experience sitting in their midst and to have a deep interest in a stupid TV documentary about the disappearance of the dinosaurs.

"Scientists believe the meteor hit the earth near what is now the Yucatán. The impact was astronomical." No. Really? And if an asteroid had hit the earth, would the impact have been meteoromical? A *Three's Company* re-run would have held more interest for her. "A cloud of dust and earth particles was sent up into the atmosphere, blocking out the warmth of the sun's rays."—not a bad piece of scientific guesswork, she thought—"gradually killing the earth's plant life, driving the earth's tempera-tures to far below freezing, possibly even spewing a layer of radioactive matter across the earth's surface." Who cared? She wanted to go back to bed.

She slipped her hand into the pocket of the cotton robe she was wearing, the tips of her fingers touching her mother's letter. Even her mother wouldn't subject her to this sort of torment, she thought, her eyes growing heavy with fatigue despite the fact that she'd slept half the af-ternoon away after her shower.

Everything was so confusing. And it was so difficult to think clearly. It was obvious, to her, if not to anyone else—namely Kurt—that her brain was recovering much more slowly than the rest of her. There were the strange new wonderful feelings she had for Kurt to sort out and decipher. Her mother. Andropov-B. Getting well. The future. People dying in Chad, the Ukraine, and Yucatán. Now the dinosaurs. Too much for one sickly little brain.

Her eyes closed, remained closed too long, and she forced them open. If only she could hold a single di-lemma in her head for more than a second or two with-out the invasion of the others, maybe she could figure out one clear answer at a time. . . .

In matching off-the-shoulder leopardskin cocktail dresses with simple seashell accessories—not unlike those worn by Betty and Wilma—she and her mother cowered in fear as they watched first one then another purple brontosaurus fall over dead from starvation. The dream-fogged air around them was thick with dust, it was difficult to see, and yet time and again her mother would put her hand across Mack's eyes to shield her from the atrocious sight, to protect her from realizing that their world was coming to an end.

Over and over she would push her mother's hand away, knowing that she needed to see what was happening in order to save them both from extinction. Realizing that the ground beneath them had stopped reverberating after the collapse of each giant beast, they stepped cautiously from the safety of their cave. It was snowing and cold. The lush jungle around them—something on the order of Kurt's greenhouse—was devastated. Everything was dead. There was nothing to eat. No, wait.

In the planting troughs in the middle of the jungle were hundreds of rice plants. She and her mother looked at one another, reading each other's thoughts. Where there was rice there was riz à l'impératrice for dessert!

Excited and hopeful, they approached the troughs, their stomachs growling—very unladylike—with hunger. They laughed, deciding nonverbally that nothing else mattered anymore but their survival. They hugged. Life was good. Life was better than before all the dinosaurs had died. And with only the two of them to make up the rules of society, life around the dead jungle was going to be very different from now on.

That's when Kurt came running at them, his fig leaf rumpled, ragged, unstarched, and so darling. He was shouting, horrified, waving his arms and pointing at huge wormlike creatures crawling out of three of the potted rice plants inside the trough. They were like something out of an old Japanese sci-fi movie, only they were real, and Kurt could understand what they were saying. He translated for her that they were crying in pain and they were angry, that they were normally very nice worms, but burned with radiation as they were, there was no telling what they might do.

And while they discussed the possibilities, her mother—starving and ignorant to the dangers of radiation, and apparently blind to the huge gooey oozing blistered worms—started eating the rice. Within seconds, she fell to the ground, bleeding from every orifice. She was hemorrhaging to death, and Kurt kept calling to the worms, "Boris. Boris." But the worms ignored him, slithering closer and closer to her mother, deadly and extremely pissed off because no one was trying to ease their pain.

It was up to Mack to save her mother and cure the worms and calm Kurt down so they could all be happy. She knelt beside her mother, scooping the blood up in her hands, trying to put it back inside her body, the worms inching closer and closer, Kurt jumping up and down in frustration and fear.

She glanced over her shoulder. A worm glared back at her, its mouth open, fangs hanging down like a venomous snake. She screamed. . . .

"Mack. Honey, wake up," she heard Kurt's much calmer voice calling her from somewhere outside the jungle. "It's a dream. Wake up. You're safe." She went running to find him, opened her eyes, and flung her arms around his neck, gasping.

"The radiation got them," she said. "From the meteor. They're in pain."

"Who? Mack, wake up. You're still dreaming."

Maybe. But he felt as real in her arms as the worm on her shoulder had.

"Where's my mother?" she asked him suddenly.

"At her hotel. Sleeping. You can call her in the morning to make sure, if you want. Was she in your dream?"

"The worms ate her, I think."

"Ugh." Clearly the psychological wounds of their relationship were deeper than he'd imagined.

It came to her slowly that she was safe in Kurt's arms, there were no worms, and her mother wasn't even in the room. She remembered the dinosaur documentary and now she was in bed. Maybe she had been asleep. Maybe it wasn't real. Maybe it was just a dream.

He gave her a drink of water and got back into the cot beside hers, lying on his side to face her. He talked about strange dreams he'd had and how real they sometimes seemed and, in general, just talked to ease her weary mind.

When his words slurred together and no longer made sense, she opened her eyes and watched him fight off sleep for a minute or two before succumbing. He was quite possibly the dearest, sweetest man of her acquaintance, she decided, loving him more than she'd ever dreamed she could love someone.

Slipping her hand out from under his, she slowly sat up and reached to the foot of the cot for her robe. Taking her mother's letter from the pocket, she placed it under her pillow and fell asleep trying to remember every word.

Kurt was always the first to take his shower, waking before any of the others. She was sitting on the edge of the cot waiting for him when he came out of the bathroom.

"I'm sorry," he said, eyeing her carefully. "Did I wake you?"

"No. I just woke up. I was wondering, would you

mind hanging around for a few minutes while I take one of those? In case I'm not as strong as I feel this morning?"

"You feel strong?" he asked, pleased. "Great. I guess I can handle another shower."

"No. I meant, just be around in case I fall or something. I'm pretty sure I can manage it alone."

"You're sure? I really don't mind. In fact, I was hoping we could make a habit of it."

He was trying to make accepting help as easy on her as possible. She smiled at him, then interrupted.

"We *will* make a habit of it, when it's more fun for both of us," she said. "But for simple hygienic purposes, it's quicker alone."

"Okay," he said, with a good-humored chuckle. He was about to help her stand up when she waved him away. "But I promise to be on my best behavior if you want to change your mind."

"I hate your best behavior," she lied, making light of the effort it took to walk to him. "I like you better scowling and persnickety and acting like a spoiled brat."

"Everybody likes me better that way. I'm only being nice to you because it annoys you."

"I'm aware of that, so you can stop it now." She used his chest for balance as she stretched up on tiptoe to kiss him with great affection. "I plan to recover my strength in spite of all your annoying niceness."

He put his hands on her hips, pulling her against him, and kissed her back. His kiss went beyond affection to desire and need. "I don't care how you do it. Just do it soon."

His sense of one-upmanship was inspiring.

Though she needed more help than she wanted to

admit, she refused to go back to bed after her shower, demanding that her breakfast be served with the others.

The doctor came to call before the trays were taken away.

"Thurman," Polly said, when he entered the outer office, masked, gowned, and gloved to avoid contamination. It sounded like a grand announcement, something like "Almighty king and ruler! All rise." However, she was the only one to stand and meet him at the door. "Goodness, don't you look nice today. That is to say, I'm sure you must under all that, your eyes are quite bright and lovely today."

"Thank you." The doctor glanced about at what was by now an avid audience. "How are you feeling this morning, Polly?"

"Very well, thank you." To everyone's delight, she blushed and simpered at him. "My goodness, those flowers are beautiful. Are they from you?"

"Ah, yes," he said, clearing his throat. "I thought perhaps you might enjoy them." Then catching himself, he added, "I thought you might all enjoy them. Oh! And there's my patient, sitting up, looking fit."

Now wouldn't you think that his patient would be the *first* thing a doctor would notice? Mack glanced at Kurt, and his expression told her that while she had taken the doctor's visits for granted and paid very little attention to the man behind the mask, Polly had looked forward to his appearances and paid a great deal of attention.

"Gracious, yes. Isn't she doing wonderfully?" Polly followed him over to Mack's chair. "Though as you can see, she's still quite weak and may continue to be for some time. Naturally, she'll need your expert observation until she's completely recovered. Overall, we're very pleased with her progress."

By now Mack's smile was something more than an act of recognition and appreciation, it was knowing and highly amused.

"Yes, indeed, you look to be in fine fettle this morning," the doctor said, his brown eyes warm and kindly.

"And I appreciate all you've done to help get me this way," Mack said.

"He's a wonderful doctor, dear."

"I can see that, Polly. He seems to have had a wonderful effect on all of us."

"Oh my, yes. He's quite wonderful."

Forevermore, the man's name would be Dr. Wonderful in Mack's mind. Imagine, a man who could dethrone dear dead Andrew in Polly's heart. Imagine three separate love affairs instigated by one Friday-the-thirteenth accident. Imagine further, if you will, the odds of anything like this ever happening again. . . .

"Let's make a deal," Mack said after lunch that afternoon. "I'll rest for a while if you'll call Eugene and ask him to get me some information on meteors and dinosaurs."

Kurt tossed her robe to the end of the cot and straightened to look down at her. "Meteors and dinosaurs? What for?"

"I'm not sure," she said, loath to tell him that her nightmare the night before was weighing heavy on her mind. "Curiosity. Something to do."

He palmed her forehead. "You're not getting weird and delirious again, are you?"

"No."

He studied her for a moment or two. "What about

your mother? Have you given any thought to calling her?"

"Some."

"Well?" he asked when she said no more. "Are you going to?"

"Probably. Eventually. I'm trying to decide what to say to her."

He shook his head, his expression stuck somewhere between anger and disappointment. "You're acting like a spoiled brat," he said, holding the sheets up for her to get under them.

It was on the tip of her tongue to tell him that it took a spoiled brat to know a spoiled brat, but that would have proved his statement.

"I don't *know* what to say to her," she amended, not liking his disapproval or having to admit he was right.

He sat down next to her, seeming to understand—as only a fellow spoiled brat might, she supposed.

"She took the first step with the letter. Now it's your turn. Call her. She'll take the next step by saying something, then it'll be your turn again. That's the way it works. One step at a time." It was more to think about, as if she didn't have enough already. He kissed her on the mouth now that her fever blisters were healed and instructed her to sleep on it.

She tried, but when the huge bubbly worms crawled back into her dreams she came awake with a start and couldn't go back to sleep. She lay there for a while thinking about them, trying to decode the meaning of the dream, but to no avail. Unless, of course, it had something to do with the consequences of buying mother-daughter off-the-shoulder leopardskin dresses.

Laughter in the outer office aroused her curiosity. Getting up and putting on her robe alone had her looking smug and self-reliant by the time she opened the door and stepped out to join in the fun. They were playing cards.

"Who's losing?" she asked, walking slowly to Kurt's side, glancing down at his fistful of red cards.

"I am," he said. "They're teaching me how to lose at hearts. Do you know anything about this game?"

"Not much. My mother's the cardplayer in our family," she said, fairly certain that red cards weren't the ones to keep. "What time is it?"

"A little after three, dear," Polly answered while Kurt concentrated. "How was your nap?"

"Fine," Mack said absently, her mind elsewhere. "Isn't it a little early for cards?"

"No way, man," Dwayne said, not looking up, his expression keen and calculating, his fingers twitching for a cigarette. "This is war. He bet us he could beat us at any card game we chose. Yesterday we taught him poker, and he cleaned up. If he's figured out how to shoot the moon, this'll be four games in a row, man."

"We taught him Old Maid and Go Fish on Monday and Tuesday," Joanne informed her—in case she was wondering.

But what Mack was wondering was how any work was getting done on Andropov-B if Andropov-K was playing cards all day?

"You stopped looking," she said suddenly. She was instantly angry and hurt.

Kurt looked at the others, who were all looking at him, then turned his head to look at Mack. He'd seen this aspect of her before.

"Let it go, Mack," he said, turning back to his cards. "I tried and I failed. I looked for a cause and I failed again. It's over, let it go."

"You're giving up?"

"I had two great shots at a dream. That's more than most people get."

"Your first shot was sabotaged, and you haven't finished the second one. There's still time to find out what went wrong and correct it."

"No," he said flatly. "People are dead. I ran out of time weeks ago. Whose turn is it?"

"But . . . have you told anyone?" She looked at the others and couldn't find one honest gaze to meet hers. "You sent a report to the CDC, didn't you? After I specifically told you not to." No answer. "Didn't you?"

He turned in his chair to face her.

"It's a lethal organism. It was killing people. Someone had to put a stop to it."

"It wasn't killing any *more* people. Those three hot zones were already isolated, and the rice there is quarantined. Do you really think I'd intentionally put more lives in jeopardy? For what? Your reputation? Your pride? Hardly. The CDC will outlaw the bacteria completely without knowing why it mutated or if it mutated anywhere else. If the mutation is isolated to those three places, you're condemning this planet to the toxic by-products of hundreds of millions of tons of fertilizers, needlessly. There's still a ninety-seven percent chance that A-B1 will work beautifully everywhere *but* those three locations."

"I couldn't take that chance."

"It wasn't your choice to make. I've been telling you that since I got here. You simply created the bacteria, then you gave it to the world. Once that happened the choices became mine, *not yours*."

"You were sick. Delirious."

"And you were full of self-pity." They glared at each

other accusingly. "It was easier to blow it off than to risk finding out that it was a total failure. That *you* were a total failure." She hesitated, but wasn't wise enough to stop herself. "Is that how it is with you, Kurt? When something goes wrong, you simply blow it off? Forget it and go on? I guess I should feel lucky you stuck it out with me, huh?"

The pain and anger in his eyes before he lowered them away from her was devastating. She'd gone too far, and now she was more alone and lonely than ever before.

It was in her heart to apologize immediately. To beg his forgiveness, to take back every word she'd said. Trouble was—and it didn't happen that often to be confused with something else—she was right.

Amazingly, they managed to avoid each other in such cramped quarters. She confined herself to Kurt's office, climbing the chain of command at the Centers for Disease Control by phone, begging for additional time, promising everything but her firstborn child that delaying any official action or public announcements would be well worth the risk.

Lucy made a kindly attempt to take her meals with Mack, but Mack sent her away, branded her a distraction. Lucy left her patient picking at her food and shuffling through piles of Dr. Andropov's papers and notes.

And it was Polly who came to sleep in the third cot in the office at night.

"No, dear, don't worry your head," she said, getting ready for bed. "That light won't bother me a bit. You know me, I sleep like the dead."

"I guess he's still pretty mad, huh?" Polly raised her brows and gave her a regretful grimace. She blew a big sad sigh from puffed-up cheeks. "I wish someone would invent a cure for a big mouth."

"Goodness, gracious. Wouldn't that be something?" Polly sent Mack an empathetic smile. "Good night, dear."

Lucy, too, turned her back to the light and fell fast asleep, leaving Mack with her scores of reports, her guilty conscience, and a burning certainty that she could save a microorganism that had a usefulness far greater than its size.

And, of course, avoiding someone didn't necessarily mean you didn't see them from time to time, watching you work from the doorway, scowling, turning away when you happened to glance up and catch his eye. . . .

"Hello. I'm calling for Julianne McKissack. I believe she has a room there," Mack said, desperation driving her to the sound of a familiar, dissociated voice. Maybe desperation did give courage to the weak. Maybe her mother was still feeling bad enough to lend her some encouragement. Mack grimaced, feeling contrite. Kurt was right. Her mother had made a first step. This was hers and she couldn't—wouldn't—purposely make it in the wrong direction. "Oh," she said when the operator came back on the line. "No, I don't want to leave voice mail, just tell her that her daughter called, please. Thank you."

She hung up the phone and stared at the jumble of papers and slides around her.

Reviewing the recent slides Kurt had made of A-B1 during the second and into the third generation from the contaminated sites in Africa, Central America, and western Russia was disheartening. She recalled Polly's comment about the cell walls looking blistered and burned, and they did. In fact, she'd shuddered when the pathetic mutated A-B1 bacteria turned up looking remarkably like the creatures of her dreams. She reviewed each soil analysis carefully. Mother Nature's kitchen, clean as a whistle. No single, double, or combination of chemicals or minerals would have such an effect on even the most delicate specimen— and A-B1 was a hardy little bugger that could withstand a great deal of interference before its integrity was violated.

Kurt had been right about Andropov-B too.

She rubbed her face as if it were made of rubber and pushed her hair back out of her eyes. She sighed and, for the first time in what seemed like hours, looked up from her work space.

Kurt was leaning against the doorjamb, watching her.

"Hi," she said, testing the waters.

"Hi." He pushed himself over to the other side of the doorjamb. "Find anything?"

She shook her head and looked away, disinclined to voice the word or to watch the satisfaction on his face.

The silence between them could have shattered windows, if there were any. Her nerves were cracking under the pressure.

"You really are one of those extremely stubborn women, aren't you, Doctor?" he said finally.

"I can be," she said softly, letting her eyes tell him that she didn't want to be; that she needed his help; that she hated the distance between them.

He walked to the other side of the worktable, his gaze never leaving her face. "Well," he said with great superiority—after three days of treating her as if she were nothing more than a pesky fly on the wall. "I'm not. I happen to be a flexible, easy-to-get-along-with, immensely magnanimous man." He made a small gesture toward the microscope. "It doesn't make any sense, does it?"

"No." Her mouth stretched to a wide smile, her heart stretched to fill her chest. "It doesn't make any sense at all. A spontaneous change isn't called for, and there's nothing in the soil to cause it. Unless it's the plants."

He was shaking his head. "IR-8. All of it. If it were the plant, half the world would be dead by now."

She folded her arms across her chest and sighed, her body sagging with defeat. "Maybe you were right. Maybe there is no answer. Maybe it just—"

"No," he said, stopping her. "You were right about that. It doesn't make sense, and it should. There has to be a reason." He held up one finger like a sword. "But I'm not a quitter. I've been at this a hell of a lot longer than you have."

"I know. And I'm sorry."

"And I'm never giving up on you," he added, as a matter of fact. "Together, the two of you don't make a thimbleful of sense, but you're my woman and that's my . . . bug, and I'm going to figure you both out if it kills me."

She grinned and put both feet on the floor. Stretching over the counter space, she puckered up for a kiss.

"I suppose you want to kiss and make up now?" he asked.

"Please? I hate it when you're angry with me."

He kissed her, quick and light. "Then don't make me mad anymore."

"I promise." He kissed her better for that, knowing full well it was a promise she wasn't likely to keep. But with intent being three fourths of the act, and with her looking at him the way she was, and considering the miserable sleepless nights he'd spent on the couch—that now fit Polly better than it fit him—it was good enough for him.

He stepped around the counter to stand beside her. He opened a notebook, flipped several pages, and closed it again.

"I called your mother this morning," he said, scratching his ear with one finger, looking sheepish, though he hadn't made any rash promises not to make *her* mad. When she looked at him, stunned, he tried to explain. "I'm sorry, I like her. I thought she deserved to know you were okay and I . . . I thought she could tell me the best way to . . . make up with you."

She looked away, across the room. The flash of temper she felt was just that, a flash, promptly replaced with curiosity.

"What'd she tell you?"

"Not much. She regretted that she couldn't be of much help to me. She said you generally blow up and get over it, but that you could hold a grudge like a pit bull hangs on to a chuck roast."

"A chuck roast? She said a chuck roast?"

"No, she said you had a *tendency* to hold a grudge. I said chuck roast."

"Never misquote my mother," she warned him. "Nothing she says is more important than the way she says it."

"Yes, ma'am."

"And what'd you tell her about me?"

"I said you were moody as hell."

"Well, wouldn't you be if someone kept going behind your back, doing your job, calling your mother."

She wasn't nearly as vexed as she sounded, and he could tell.

"You were too sick to do it yourself. Someone—"

"I'm not sick anymore."

"Then do your own job and call your own mother."

"I did."

"You did?"

"Yes."

"Well? How'd it go?"

"She wasn't in." She looked away, then turned back to him. "You know, you'd better promise to stop making me mad too."

He looked her straight in the eye and lied. "I promise."

She tried to cling to anything that halfway resembled censure or at the very least a firm resolve not to tolerate further intrusions into her affairs, but his lips were twitching and his eyes were twinkling with the undeniable knowledge that they'd be meddling in each other's lives until day one or both of them died.

"Nap time!" Kurt announced for the third and last time that afternoon. If Mack ignored him again, he'd pick her up and throw her in bed.

"But I'm not tired."

"But it doesn't matter. Thurman says a relapse is entirely possible—ask Polly. I think she wrote it down."

"She writes down everything he says," she grumbled, keeping her eye to the microscope. "Wouldn't surprise me if she started chiseling every word he utters in stone."

"Thurman is a fine physician."

"So I've heard and heard and heard."

"I rather like the way she hangs on his every word and follows him around like a second shadow."

"You would."

He chuckled. "I take it you'd be unwilling to take lessons from her."

She looked up then. "You take it correctly. Between Polly and Thurman, and the way Joanne adores Dwayne as if he were the Second Coming or something, somebody has to wet down some of the male ego around here or we'll suffocate."

"But why does it have to be *my* ego?" he asked, bending at the waist to whine in her face.

She palmed his stubbled cheeks. "Because everyone already knows that you're the smartest, biggest, handsomest, funniest, most generous man in the world, and that you have plenty of ego to spare."

He frowned. Was that a hit or a kiss?

He got his answer when she laid a hot one smack on his mouth.

"Now I'm really going to make you take a nap."

She laughed. "Only if you take it with me."

His eyes narrowed suspiciously. "A real nap. Rest. Sleep."

"I can't sleep," she said, thirty minutes later. They'd started out on the cots facing each other, rolled over with their backs to each other, and now she rolled over to face him again.

"Me either," he said, meeting her gaze.

"What'll we do now?"

"Lock the doors?"

"We have to get up soon," Mack mumbled into her pillow, her eyes closed, every muscle of her naked body kneaded to a doughy consistency from the slow, gentle finger massage Kurt was giving her. "Even Polly's naps aren't this long."

"They would be if she was taking them with Thurman."

She made a sound as if he'd kicked the air out of her. He laughed, and she felt the hair on his chest tickle at her ribs.

"I know. It's like trying to picture your favorite grandmother having sex."

An equally eerie picture—her mother having sex. Funny thing about that photo, her mother was only seventeen years her senior, and she wasn't having any trouble seeing herself making love with Kurt in twenty years. Or thirty years. Or . . .

"What should I say if she calls back?"

"Who?"

"Mother."

"Well, don't call her mother like that. Just say hello."

"Then what?"

"I'm fine. How are you?"

"And she'll take it from there?"

"I would imagine so. I told her you were still stuporous and dull-witted. She isn't expecting much."

She turned her head over on the pillow to face him. He had his fist stuck in his cheek to hold up his head.

"Sometimes I really hate you a lot."

He laughed, leaning forward to kiss her below the ear. "I know. Ain't hate great?"

They were dressed and ready to attack together the biggest single question confronting them. Not the future. Not their love for each other, but why the heck was Andropov-B mutating? When the phone in the outer office rang, they both turned to stare at the quiet phone on the corner of Kurt's big desk, the light coming on, then flashing on hold.

"That's her," she said, knowing her mother's ring instinctively.

"Be nice." He nudged her toward the phone as he answered Joanne's meek tapping at the door.

"Hello?" Mack said into the receiver, watching Kurt backing Joanne and himself out the door. "Hello, ah, Mama."

Mama? he mouthed with a sickened expression.

She's Southern, she mouthed back with a shrug.

Then she shook her head at Kurt, grinned, and said, "I'm fine. How are you?"

He returned her smirk and closed the door.

THIRTEEN

That night Mack and her mother debated the merits of panther pelts and lion manes versus faux furs from Sabatini's in New York. Mange and availability seemed to be the highlights of the discussion, until the huge purple brontosauruses began to fall once more, shaking the earth, shattering eardrums with their cries of hunger. From that point on, her nightmare was much the same as before, but this one had a surprise ending.

Once again the pain-crazed worms slithered from the potted plants of rice in the trough, situated in the center of the dead greenhouselike jungle, and once again her famished mother ate the plants and fell over bleeding. Mack rushed to her side and began scooping up the blood, failing and flustered with her attempts to restore her mother's life. But wait! When she glanced over her shoulder at the ferocious worm glaring into her eyes and started screaming, her mother—calm, cool, and collected as ever—sat up, no longer faking death, to distract the evil, venomous worms from her daughter. In her hands she had a large jar of very expensive antiwrinkle cream, which she quickly opened and began to slather on the worm clinging to Mack's shoulder.

Naturally, the worm dewrinkled instantly, and became as soft and smooth as . . . as a normal worm. It even began to shrink. Though she never actually moved her lips, except to display an I-told-you smile, she heard her mother saying, "Didn't I tell you that all any woman really needs is a good antiwrinkle cream to protect her youthful complexion from the harmful effects of the sun's rays?"

That's when she knew. . . .

She was instantly awake, alert, and clear-eyed. Kurt, sleeping like a dead man, arms flung wide, one leg hanging off the cot, was oblivious to her earth-rocking revelation, and she decided to leave him that way—for the moment.

As quiet as an eel in oil, she closed the door on Polly's snoring in the outer office. Then she stood in the dark and silently screamed in excitement. It was like being the first to figure out that the murderer was Professor Plum in the conservatory with the wrench. She knew actually what the killer was.

She was the winner.

Now all she had to do was prove it.

Turning on the lamp near the phone, she realized that the light was bright and could, possibly, be seen from the greenhouse. From the coatrack beside the office door, she snatched Kurt's lab jacket and draped it over the lamp and the phone and her head to dull the light.

"Eugene?" she said moments later, her voice one decibel higher than a whisper. "I'm sorry to wake you. . . . I said, I'm sorry to wake you at this hour, but there's something very important. . . . Oh. This is Mack. Dr. McKissack? . . . I do? Well, why would you be expecting Lucy to call at this time of night? . . . No, I hadn't realized she had trouble sleeping at night. . . . So, she calls you? To talk . . . No. As far as I know she's fine. We're all fine. . . . Well, let me think. She's very nice, very kind. She has sort of greenish eyes, I guess, and blond hair and a friendly smile. Average height and build . . . Oh, she's probably in her midthirties. . . . Why are you asking all these questions about her?"

As if she didn't know. The "heart condition" that had infected everyone in quarantine was now running rampant through the building. She could hear the symptoms in his voice.

"Well, it is important, but it doesn't have anything to do with the quarantine really. I need you to get me some information as quickly as you can. . . . Okay. I need a world atlas. I also need a detailed mineral map of Africa, specifically Chad, if you can find one; Central America, primarily the Yucatán, and another one of western Russia and the Ukraine. And I want everything you can dig up for me on radiation poisoning. How long do you think that will take you? . . . Yes, I'm sorry. I need it now. . . . Good . . . Oh, you bet I will. The minute she wakes up. Thanks, Eugene."

Crawling out from under the lab jacket, she went in search of Kurt's specimen ledger, where the letters and numbers neatly labeled on each of the rice plants in the greenhouse would add up to real facts and specific places.

Eugene faxed what information he could find on such short notice ninety minutes later. Gnawing on a pencil, notes and lab reports flying about like leaves in the wind, Mack recollected exactly what it was she loved about her job. Her blood was boiling with the thrill of victory. She felt a kinship with every cop who had ever nabbed a bad guy; every doctor who had ever made an accurate diagnosis; every lawyer who had ever won a righteous case; every speedster who had ever won a race; every woman who had ever given birth; every crossword fanatic who had ever solved a puzzle.

She put her fists to her mouth and sucked in a scream of exhilaration that would have deafened a banshee. She couldn't stand it any longer, she decided, hopping off the stool and skip-leaping back into the office to wake Kurt.

"Shhh. You'll wake Lucy," she murmured in his face when he would have protested. "Get up. If you thought you loved me yesterday, wait till you hear what I've done."

Not a morning man, Kurt groused low in his throat, but stumbled out into the lab behind her.

She closed the door behind him, took his arm, and dragged him toward the work counter. "It came to me in a dream. It made so much sense, I wanted to knock myself out for not thinking of it sooner."

"What?"

"Well, it started with my mother and her anti-wrinkle cream, but that didn't have anything to do with it really because it was the worms all along. . . ."

"You had a dream about worms and antiwrinkle cream?"

"It was a nightmare, really. My mother's best dress had mange and the dinosaurs were dying like flies." She laughed and kissed him for the expression on his face. "It was the worms all along. They weren't worms. They were microbes. They were like atomic Andropov-Bs . . . from the radiation that was scattered over the face of the earth when the meteor hit and killed all the dinosaurs."

Stunned, he stared at her. She looked flushed and

feverish, but the truth of it was, he simply didn't want to know if she was sick again. His heart couldn't take it.

"Wake up," she said, snapping her fingers in front of his eyes. "I know why A-B1 mutated."

"Mack, honey, have you been taking your pills?"

"Kurt. Kurt," she said, framing his face with her hands. "You are so *cute* and I love you *so* much, but if you don't pay attention, I'm going to hit you. Look. Come here and look at this. See here, see where the four soil samples from Chad were taken from?" He bent over the pile of papers and then nodded. "And see here? This is where the only contaminated sample came from, this place here. Look. Look here," she said excitedly, waving a mineral map under his nose. "There's a uranium mine not ten miles from the sample site."

When he failed to dance a jig at this news, it became apparent that he was going to need a little more convincing.

"Okay. Coincidence, you say. Well, this next one was pure brilliance on my part. Look. Here in the Ukraine outside Kiev and here again in Prypiat, both sites are well within the hundred-mile fallout radius of Chernobyl."

Now she had his attention.

"The Yucatán is a stretch. There's no mine and no nuclear reactor, but how far wrong can several thousand paleontologists be? If a meteor did hit there and did pull radioactive matter into our atmosphere with it, that could do it. Even if it's barely detectable now, trace amounts of radiation could do it eventually. Couldn't it? I mean, it might not affect the people living there, but if they were tiny bacteria, buried in the contaminated soil there for three years, with no previous exposure to enable them to build up any sort of tolerance to the radiation, couldn't that do it?"

He was thinking.

"And look here. The symptoms fit. In moderate-to-high doses it takes two to four weeks to die. Vomiting, diarrhea, fever, hemorrhage, rapid emaciation. Even with low doses, if it goes untreated, the symptoms are the same. It fits, Kurt. It all fits."

He sat down on the stool she'd been sitting on most of the night and scanned the data, barely seeing it, his brain was so full of possibilities.

"We don't have a detector here. We'll have to send the samples out," he said, deep in thought.

"Sure. And I'll fly a truckload of geologists down to the Yucatán the day the quarantine lifts."

"No. Someone else'll have to go. We can't wait that long."

Disgruntled, she looked somewhat like a deflated bulldog. "But I'm the one . . . it's my theory. . . ."

He looked at her, his eyes bright with hope, his lips curled with satisfaction and delight.

"You certainly are, and it sure is, and I think you're terrific."

Over*in*flated bulldog.

"Yeah?"

"Yeah. Very terrific." He reached out for her waist, pulling her between his legs and as close as he could get her. "You've saved my life."

"Oh no."

"The day you walked off that elevator and stuck your chin out at me, I knew my life would never be the same. And now you've saved Andropov-B." He stopped short as a simple thought occurred to him. "Why, I think you must be my lucky penny."

"Ugh."

❦———————❦

They fried the lines of communication to the CDC and the World Health Organization and to Dick Preston and Kurt's mom . . . and even to Mack's mama that morning.

"She actually sounded sort of interested," Mack said, sounding as perplexed as she was pleased. "Asked me all sorts of questions. Hmmph."

"Could it be this is the first time you've ever tried to tell her about what you do?" Kurt asked mildly, tossing his dirty scrubs into the red laundry bag after his shower. He stepped back into the bathroom to comb his hair.

"Could be," she said thoughtfully. And a few seconds later she added, "You know, you make it sound as if this . . . thing between me and my mother is all my fault. I would have told her, if she'd ever asked, you know."

"I know." He turned the light out as he joined her in the office/bedroom.

"Up until almost three weeks ago, my job was my life, and she never once asked about it."

"Maybe up until almost three weeks ago your life sounded so dull, it wasn't worth asking about."

Taking immediate umbrage, she gasped and started to dispute him before she saw the teasing humor in his eyes and the rather absurd grin on his face.

"Do you have to special-order aspirin for that big head of yours?"

"Nope," he said, sitting beside her on the cot, leaning back next to her against the wall and lacing his fingers over his stomach, imitating her. "I never get headaches."

"Too busy giving them to someone else?"

He shook his head. "Too busy loving you. All I have to do is think about you, and my head is so full, there's no room for a headache."

"You have the prettiest blue eyes I've ever seen," she said, caught tight in them.

"And you are the easiest woman I've ever known," he said, teasing her. "A little flattery and you fall like a ton of bricks."

"Oh yeah?" she said, giving him the ultimate comeback in any dispute.

"Yeah." The ultimate answer. "All I have to do to shut you up is tell you that I love the way your hair skims across your neck here," he said, leaning over her to brush the dark swag of hair back with one finger, purposely grazing her throat with the tip, and placing a kiss in the general vicinity of where it had been. "And you melt like butter in the sun."

Okay. That was true.

"And if I say I love the way your eyelashes curl up at the corners here . . . and here." He kissed both corners to close her eyes. "You hold your breath."

All right. That was true too.

"And if I say I love the way you taste." He licked her lips with the tip of his. "And if I touch you here . . ." He slid his hand effortlessly under her top to cup her breast. "Well, then you tremble like a woman in need and, yes, that's right, you put your arms around me and try to kiss me, just like this. . . ."

He was such a damned know-it-all!

Of course he was omitting what all this was doing to *him*. The low hungry groan in his throat may have been a feeble effort at it, but he was more specific with his actions. Kissing her until she was languid enough to be laid back against the bed; pushing her top and bra up to expose her breasts to his mouth; making light work of the scrub bottoms when she bowed her back, twisting with desire.

A knock at the door had them all arms and legs, trying to sit up and appear nonchalant as the doorknob started to rattle before opening.

"Hey, man. You busy?" Dwayne popped his head into the room.

"Yes, I'm busy," Kurt said with a growl. "We're both busy."

"No. No, we're not busy. We . . . we were just talking," she said, sticking an elbow in Kurt's ribs.

"Good. I need to talk, too, man." Dwayne entered the room and closed the door as if he'd been invited. "And actually, I need to talk to both of you, maybe. A woman's viewpoint can't hurt."

"Are you kidding?" Kurt rolled his eyes.

"No. Man, I'm serious." Dwayne sat down on the cot opposite them. "I don't think I've ever been this serious about anything ever in my whole life. I mean, I know what I want, I'm just not sure if what I want is the right thing to want, you know?"

"No. Think out your thoughts before you speak and get specific."

Taking no offense, as he was, by now, accustomed to Kurt's brief but frequent fits of temper, Dwayne simply nodded and tried to focus his thoughts. "I want to get married," he said.

"You want to what?"

"Get married, man. To Joanne. We both want to get married. To each other."

The look on Kurt's face was indescribable. Mack's was no better. And they were both speechless.

"What do you think?" Dwayne looked from one to the other of them.

They looked at each other, nonplussed, then back at Dwayne.

"Well . . ." Kurt said, stumped.

"Gee, Dwayne . . ." Mack began.

"I know what you're thinking," he said—which was a good thing, because they sure didn't. "You're thinking I'm too weird to get married. That I'm too irresponsible and Joanne is too good for me and I don't have a job now 'cuz Myrna hates me and won't let me work for her brother anymore, not that I want anything to do with the bio-transporting business anymore anyway, but I also don't have a place to live if I have to move out of Myrna's place and Joanne's parents are going to think I'm a bum now and . . . and everything. Maybe we shouldn't get married, you know?"

Yes, yes. That about covered everything they were thinking.

"Trouble is," Dwayne went on without pause, "this whole thing . . . with the bugs and the doc here getting sick and almost dying and all, well, it makes me think that none of that other stuff really matters. You know? I mean, compared to dying, getting married doesn't seem so bad. No matter what."

"Well, putting it that way, you're right," Kurt said, moving from shock to amusement.

Mack, however, was not amused. Marriage was a serious business. There hadn't been one in *her* family for two generations.

"No," she said, shaking her head. "You were right the first time. Getting married right now is a bad idea."

As it was generally the woman who favored the state

of matrimony, the two men turned to stare at her in confusion.

"Think about it. You hardly know each other. How can you be sure that you're really in love under these circumstances? Being in intense, dangerous situations can play tricks on your emotions. Sometimes you do or think things you wouldn't think or do under normal circumstances. And . . . and a job and a home aren't the only things you need to consider with marriage. What about children? You're both so young and Joanne is in school. A baby would ruin everything, your whole life. I strongly advise against it."

Dwayne looked to Kurt for the advice he *really* wanted, and Mack looked to him for agreement. But Kurt was frowning and thoughtful, offering no advice at all.

"Have you talked to anyone else about this?" she asked while they waited for Kurt to make up his mind and say something. "Polly? Or Joanne's parents? Or your parents?"

"Polly's a pretty smart old girl. We could ask her, but Joanne's folks and my folks . . . I don't know. They wouldn't understand all this."

"All what?"

"What's happened to us. What we've been through." Dwayne looked at the clasped hands between his knees, then looked up with a compelling need to make her understand. "It's like . . . when you got sick, you know? Joanne was scared. Scared for you, but scared she'd get it too. And I was scared." He shook his head in wonder. "She cried. And she wanted me to hold her, so I did. No one's ever done that before, you know? Made me feel like I could protect her, maybe. And the way she talks to me, like I know stuff and what I do is okay . . . I don't know. I feel different, you know? Like maybe I could protect her. Maybe I could do something right." He shook his head. "Man, she thinks I'm responsible and sometimes I feel like if she thinks I am, maybe I could be, you know? Maybe I wanna be."

Mack smiled. Joanne was good for Dwayne's ego. She believed in him. And he was beginning to believe in himself. That's all it took usually, that one special someone to believe in you.

"That's special, Dwayne, and I'm glad for you," she said sincerely. "But it's still not enough to base a marriage on. Maybe if you and Joanne date for a while once this is all over. Maybe once she finishes school and you—"

"Why isn't that enough for a marriage?" Kurt asked, looking at her strangely. "What more does it take? They love each other. They believe in each other. They're young and healthy and full of hope, like us. Hell, I think we should make it a double wedding."

"What?"

"Sure," he said, electrified, acting odd. "We can do it here, while we're all still in quarantine. That'll certainly make it an unforgettable occasion. We'll use Dick's speakerphone and set up a conference call between the minister and us and our mothers, and Dwayne and Joanne's folks, so they can all listen in. Oh! And Polly and Thurman. If they don't want to do the deed with us, they can be our witnesses."

"Do the deed?"

"Stellar, man," Dwayne said, standing up. "I wonder if we can get the Guinness people in on this. You know, highest number of weddings performed at one time, in quarantine? Something like that? And I bet *People* magazine would go nuts for something like this."

"That's because this *is* nuts," Mack said, hardly believing her ears. "Calm down, Dwayne, let's not get ahead of ourselves here. In fact"—she patted his chest absently—"why don't you let Kurt and me talk it through for a few minutes alone. There's plenty of time yet to decide what to do."

"Okay. I'll go tell Joanne. She'll love this," he said, leaving immediately.

She took the time to send a small mental prayer for Joanne's continued good sense and caution, then turned on Kurt. "Are you out of your mind?"

"No. Do I look it?"

"No, but you sound like it. Dwayne thinks you're serious."

"And you don't?"

"Of course I don't. We can't have a double wedding."

He knew this, and if Joanne couldn't or wouldn't dissuade Dwayne, he would—later. At present, he was far more interested in Mack's overemphatic counsel against it.

"Why not?"

She stared at him, her mind vacant.

"They're too young," she said, grasping at straws.

"We're not. We both have a job. We both have a place to live. We love each other. I believe in you."

"I believe in you too," she said weakly, knowing that inside all those truths there had to be a valid reason for a marriage between them not to work.

"We're reasonably healthy, God knows. And I'm full of hope," he said, watching her.

"Me too. I guess." She counted the square tiles on the floor. It was all her mind was good for—it wasn't feeding her any good points to argue; wasn't helping her sort out her emotions; wasn't doing anything but counting squares and sputtering futilely.

"Is it children?" he asked.

"What?"

"Don't you want children?"

"Who me?"

"It's the last point on the list. I know you said your life wasn't conducive to raising children. You said you thought about them, but you just didn't have any. Is that because you don't want any?"

"No, I . . ." She shrugged. "I don't know."

"If children weren't an issue, how would you feel?"

She looked at him straight on then. His thoughts were unfathomable, but hers were beginning to rise to the surface.

She knew two out of three marriages failed. Personally, she knew marriage to the wrong person—socially, financially, emotionally—was to be avoided at all costs; even shame, disgrace, and a lifetime of sorrow were preferable. And children? They were a burden. Even if you loved them—as she was beginning to suspect her parents had loved her all along—they were ungrateful and thoughtless and uncaring, just as she had been.

Oh, she knew all about the Brady Bunch and the Cleavers. She knew somewhere, someplace, some marriages worked or people wouldn't keep trying it; wouldn't make such a big deal of it; wouldn't wish and yearn for the right mate to build one with. But where was that place? How did one identify the right mate? Was it worth risking the pain of failure?

Children aside, how *did* she feel about marriage?

"I don't know," she said finally.

"I see," he said, his expression a stone mask before he looked away.

"No. I don't think you do understand." She sat down beside him in the midst of a self-revelation. "Unwed mothers are still deeply frowned upon where I come from, and yet my mother chose to be one rather than marry a perfectly wonderful man like my father. Does that make sense? She didn't date and she never got married because of it—or at least that was the excuse she used. And *me*, I avoided what my mother labeled eligible young men the same way I avoided roadkill. I thought it was to make her angry but . . . maybe that wasn't all of it. And when I did date, I dated bad boys, maybe . . . maybe because they scared me as much as they scared my mother. And I picked the job most likely to destroy any sort of long-term relationship. I've seen young girls sold by their families to the highest bidder, who seem perfectly content in their marriages. And I've sat in the lounge of my mother's country club and watched men cheating on their wives and lonely drunken women sitting together, laughing, pretending nothing is wrong. *You're* not what I don't know about, Kurt." She slipped her hand between the two of his whether he wanted it there or not. "You, I want to know you forever. It's marriage I don't know about—literally. I don't know what it is, or how it's supposed to work, or what it's really supposed to be." She waited until he looked at her. "Marriage was never an issue for me because I've never known enough about it to discuss it. In fact, looking back, I think I might have gone out of my way to avoid those discussions for that very reason."

He studied the deep green eyes he'd come to love so dearly, which reflected so much of what he felt back at him, and saw not only her confusion, but the truth in her soul.

"You're scared."

"I'm terrified."

His smile was small and sympathetic. "Scared, I can handle," he said, gently squeezing her fingers. "Choosing that fear over what we have together is *not* something I would handle well."

She chuckled, envisioning the pain and anger she'd narrowly averted. He caressed the curve of her cheek with the back of his hand and smiled as he tucked her hair behind her small ear.

"You're a smart woman. You should be scared," he said. "I'm not an easy person to live with." He glanced down at their intertwined fingers. "At best, I'm selfish, short-tempered, and set in my ways. But if it makes you feel any better, I'm scared too."

"Because your first marriage failed," she said. "Because you'd have to trust another woman."

His eyes narrowed in thought and he looked away. He hadn't thought of that, but now that he was thinking of it, it wasn't a problem.

"No. You are my life, so I guess I'm sort of compelled to trust you," he said, smiling, a vain attempt to make light of a serious declaration. Then he sighed. "I'm more afraid that you'll never know"—he hesitated—"that I'll never be able to show you enough how much you mean to me."

"You're doing a pretty good job of it right now." Her throat was thick with emotion. "Or . . . am I being easy again?"

He laughed then, shaking and nodding his head at once.

"Actually," he said, sobering a little, "I think a healthy dose of fear is something else every marriage should have. I assumed a lot the first time. That we wanted the same things. That she was as content as I was. But there isn't anything about a marriage that should be taken for granted. You were right about love—it's not enough. It needs constant attention. It's a lot of work. A lot of compromising and realigning of your thoughts and goals." He tangled his gaze with hers. "The thing is, Mack, I've never been able to shake the feeling that it's worth it. I want to try it again, with you."

"What about children?"

He shrugged. "Optional."

She chewed on her lower lip for a second. "Actually, I was thinking . . . I've thought that . . . I think I'd like one. All I ever wanted from my mother was love, to *know* she loved me. I think I could do that. I think I could love a baby, and somehow let it know I love it."

"I know you could."

With a few deep-seated misgivings she glanced away, hope welling in her heart. She suddenly frowned.

"Let's realign our thoughts and do some serious compromising on this double-wedding thing with Dwayne, though, shall we?"

"You don't like the idea?" he asked, being facetious. Frankly, he'd rather poke a stick in his eye.

"Well, I admit I've never dreamed of a big wedding with a white dress and cathedral, but getting married in this lab and having to share an anniversary with Dwayne and Joanne sounds like a nightmare." Then she added, "Besides, my mother would kill me."

"Nah. She won't care. She'll be too busy being grateful to have her spinster daughter off her hands . . . ugh!"

He grabbed her hands and pushed her back on the bed to escape another rib-rattling punch. With her safely pinned beneath him, he was forced to kiss her into a quiet, helpless submission.

"Okay," he said, breathless from his efforts. "We'll tell her we went a little crazy. We were feverish. We got bit by a lovebug and couldn't help ourselves. . . . Think she'll buy it?"

EPILOGUE

Mack's mother bought it—and she paid for the wedding, too, handling everything in her usual calm, efficient manner. It took place in Vicksburg, a month after they were released from quarantine with a clean bill of health.

With considerably more understanding than she'd ever had before, Mack didn't expect to see a great deal of emotion from her mother that day. And she didn't. But to see her walking tall and proud down the aisle ahead of her, to sit in the honored position of mother of the bride, brought tears to her eyes. The pride was real.

The two of them had come a long way since that summer her father had stormed Vicksburg. Perhaps they hadn't taken the easiest path or even blazed their trail in the straightest, most efficient manner imaginable, but they had arrived at their destination just the same. Two women, so different, sharing so much, knowing the other so well, loving each other so hard, that it took not gestures or words but a mere meeting of the eyes to feel the solid, distinct, unbreakable bond between them.

The reception was held at the bride's childhood

home, its gardens bulging with blossoms. The air was scented with their fragrance and Mack's deep rich memories of the delta and being with her father. Friends and neighbors arrived from all over Vicksburg to witness the honorable marriage of Julianne McKissack's illegitimate daughter, and petty though it was, Mack and Julianne both felt a sense of victory in it.

It was almost as if a wrong had been righted or the broken link in a chain had been mended. Julianne exuded a certain air of peace and satisfaction that her daughter found gratifying. And if at times Mack had doubted her mother's sense of humor, the selection—and conspicuous repetition—of The Supremes' "Love Is Like an Itching in My Heart" and George Strait's "Lovebug" as appropriate preceremony church music and reception tunes was enough to let her know it was alive and well, albeit a wee bit warped.

She even paid to have the other victims of her daughter's "fatal disease" at the wedding. . . .

"My gracious me, such a hoo-ha," Polly was heard to say. "When Thurman and I decided to shack up together, we were looking forward to fair weather. You have no idea how big a fuss twelve cats can make living with four dogs. We're ready to trade them all in for hogs."

"I don't think they'll let you keep farm animals inside the city limits," Dwayne informed her, his arm slung casually across Joanne's shoulders. His hair was cut and he was wearing a new dark blue suit—a winsome picture of his former self. He was now a college student, with a part-time job, renting a room in the home of his girlfriend's very understanding parents. "At least that's what Mr. Kriser said when I moved in with Joanne and them. . . . I had to leave my boa constrictor with

Myrna, which was all right 'cuz she always liked it more than I did anyway. She thinks there's a Tibetan monk living in it."

"I suppose that's true." Polly nodded. "About the city limits, that is. Maybe about the monk too."

"Well, I'm not too sure about that stuff anymore, myself," Dwayne said, seeming years older after one short month. "In my Philosophy 101 class that I'm taking at the community college, they don't put much stock in that superstitious stuff. Man, I tried to tell them about that Friday-the-thirteenth thing we all went through this summer, but they weren't buying any of it. According to them, it was pure coincidence. . . ."

And the newlyweds? They lived happily ever after, of course—with a little compromising and realigning of their goals, a few spats, and a great deal of patience.

And when people asked them how they met, as people are wont to do at times, they were never too sure how to answer.

You see, if coincidence is defined as the simultaneous occurrence of events or circumstances remarkable for a lack of apparent causal connection, it wasn't quite enough to explain what happened to them. And as to Friday the thirteenth being regarded as unlucky by everyone, well, that wasn't exactly how they felt either.

Generally, they'd smile at each other, shake their heads, and stick to the easiest, shortest answer that made any sense at all. . . .

They'd gotten bit by the lovebug.

THE EDITORS' CORNER

Next month LOVESWEPT brings you sizzling heroes just perfect for these sultry nights. From the heat-soaked state of Texas to the steamy city of New Orleans, the four terrific authors in our lineup sear the pages with white-hot tales of romance. So grab a cool drink and sit back—temperatures are about to skyrocket with passion.

Leanne Banks continues her bestselling Pendleton Brothers series in **FOR THE LOVE OF SIN,** LOVESWEPT #794. Troy Pendleton is too big and too rugged—well over six feet of unapologetic masculinity on a mission. He's followed Senada Calhoun all the way to Texas, and he doesn't plan on leaving without her—or the truth! A seductress whose grin could tempt a saint, Sin likes calling the shots, but Troy knows just how to touch her so she melts like chocolate in the sun. With stunning sensuality, Leanne proves just how good it feels to be just a little bad.

In **BELATED BRIDE**, LOVESWEPT #795, Charlotte Hughes tells a poignant story of love postponed but never silenced. Heartbreak and lies had driven Lucy Odum from her small town, a newborn in her arms—and only a photo of her fiancé to remember him by. But when she returns several years later, she discovers a shocking truth: Scott Bufford is alive! Shaken by what he thinks is her betrayal, yet unwilling to pretend that he doesn't hunger for her still, he must convince Lucy that the future still holds wondrous possibilities for marriage. Charlotte blends her trademark warmth and high spirits with touching tenderness for a heart-grabbing read.

Cheryln Biggs makes her LOVESWEPT debut with a tale of southern intrigue and perilous attraction in **DEVIL OF A CHANCE**, LOVESWEPT #796. Chance Reitchelle's eyes remind Kelly Garritson of midnight fog, their depths a shadowy world where a rookie private eye could get lost forever! Raised in a family of cops, she doesn't back down easily, but being paired with Chance to recover stolen horses means stakeouts in close quarters—and a sizzling surrender to the savage heat of his hands on her flesh. Cheryln has thrilled romance lovers before with novels written under the names Cheryl Biggs and Cheryln Jac—and we're so pleased to present her to you as a LOVESWEPT author.

Finally, there's **DADDY CANDIDATE**, LOVESWEPT #797, by talented newcomer Maureen Caudill. She isn't waiting a moment longer, Lyssa Cooper decides—it's time to find a husband, have a baby, and settle down. But locating the man who'd match up with her list of virtues seems impossible, until Rome Novak volunteers to help narrow the field. He knows he isn't cut out for commitment, but Lyssa's wildfire kisses and an adorable imp named Mel may soon change his mind. This is one treasure hunt with an irresistible rogue as the prize! A delightful romp from an author certain to become an instant reader favorite.

Happy reading!

With warmest wishes,

Beth de Guzman

Shauna Summers

Beth de Guzman   Shauna Summers

Senior Editor   Editor

P.S. Watch for these Bantam women's fiction titles coming in July: **MISCHIEF,** the newest hardcover from blockbuster author Amanda Quick, is guaranteed to deliver the summer's best romantic read. LOVESWEPT favorite and rising star in historical romance Sandra Chastain follows up the delightful SCANDAL IN SILK with another western treat, **RAVEN AND THE COWBOY,** in which reluctant lovers embark on a perilous quest for sacred treasure. And for those who believe in **THE MAGIC,** acclaimed newcomer Juliana Garnett returns to medieval England, where a deposed heiress with "the Sight" enlists a Crusader's help to regain her lost kingdom.

Be sure to see next month's LOVESWEPTs for a preview of these exceptional novels. And immediately following this page, preview the Bantam women's fiction titles on sale now!

Don't miss these extraordinary books
by your favorite Bantam authors!

On sale in May

VICE
by Jane Feather

THE ENGAGEMENT
by Suzanne Robinson

NIGHT MOVES
by Sandra Canfield

SWEET LOVE, SURVIVE
by Susan Johnson

From the incomparable

Jane Feather

nationally bestselling author of *Violet* and *Vanity*,
comes an enthralling new romance
of daring deception and forbidden passion

VICE

"Jane Feather is an accomplished storyteller . . .
rare and wonderful."
—*Daily News of Los Angeles*

Juliana drew the line at becoming a harlot. She had already begun the week as a bride . . . and ended it as a murderess. She was sure no one would believe that she'd hit her elderly groom with a bed warmer and knocked him dead quite by accident. So she did the only thing she could—she ran. Yet now she was in no position to turn down a shocking offer from the Duke of Redmayne: that she become one man's wife and another man's mistress— his mistress. Could she play such a role? Could she live up to such a bargain? And once she had tasted the pleasures of Redmayne's bed, would she ever want anything else?

Tarquin took the scent of his wine and examined the still figure. She reminded him of a hart at bay, radiating a kind of desperate courage that nevertheless acknowledged the grim reality of its position. Her eyes met his scrutiny without blinking, the firm chin tilted, the wide, full mouth taut. There was something uncompromising about Juliana Beresford, from the tip of that flaming head of hair to the toes of her slender feet. The image of her naked body rose unbidden in his mind. His eyes narrowed as his languid gaze slid over her, envisioning the voluptuous quality of her nudity, the smooth white skin in startling contrast to the glowing hair.

"If you insist upon making this proposition, my lord duke, I wish you would do so." Juliana spoke suddenly, breaking the intensity of a silence that had been having the strangest effect upon her. Her skin was tingling all over, her nipples pricking against her laced bodice, and she had to fight against the urge to drop her eyes from that languid and yet curiously penetrating gray scrutiny.

"By all means," he said, taking a sip of his wine. "But I must ask you a question. Are you still a virgin?"

Juliana felt the color drain from her face. She stared at him. "What business is that of yours?"

"It's very much my business," the duke said evenly. "Whether or not I make this proposition depends upon your answer."

"I will not answer such a question," Juliana declared from a realm of outrage beyond anger.

"My dear, you must. If you wish to spare yourself the inconvenience of examination," he said in the same level tone. "Mistress Dennison will discover the answer for herself, if you will not tell me."

Juliana shook her head, beyond words.

He rose from his chair and crossed the small space between them. Bending over her, he took her chin between finger and thumb and tilted her face to meet his steady gaze. "Juliana, you told Mistress Dennison that your husband died before your marriage was consummated. Is that the truth?"

"Why would I say it if it wasn't?" Somehow she still managed to sound unyielding, even as she yielded the answer because she knew she had no choice.

He held her chin for a long moment as she glared up at him, wishing she had a knife. She imagined plunging it into his chest as he stood so close to her she could smell his skin and a faint hint of the dried lavender that had been strewn among his fresh-washed linen.

Then he released her with a nod. "I believe you."

"Oh, you do me too much honor, sir," she said, her voice shaking with fury. Springing to her feet, she drove her fist into his belly with all the force she could muster.

He doubled over with a gasp of pain, but as she turned to run, he grabbed her and held on even as he fought for breath.

Juliana struggled to free her wrist from a grip like steel. She raised her leg to kick him but he swung sideways so her foot met only his thigh.

"Be still!" he gasped through clenched teeth. "Hell and the devil, girl!" He jerked her wrist hard and finally she stopped fighting.

Slowly, Tarquin straightened up as the pain receded and he could breathe again. "Hair as hot as the fires of hell goes with the devil's own temper, I suppose," he said, and to Juliana's astonishment his mouth quirked in a rueful smile, although he still held her wrist tightly. "I must bear that in mind in future."

"What do you want of me?" Juliana demanded.

"Quite simply, child, I wish you to marry my cousin, Viscount Edgecombe." He released her wrist as he said this and calmly straightened his coat and the disordered lace ruffles at his cuffs.

"You want me to do *what*?"

"I believe you heard me." He strolled away from her to refill his wineglass. "More champagne?"

Juliana shook her head. She'd barely touched what was in her glass. "I don't understand."

The duke turned back to face her. He sipped his wine reflectively. "I need a wife for my cousin, Lucien. A wife who will bear a child, an heir to the Edgecombe estate and title.

"The present heir is somewhat slow-witted. Oh, he's a nice enough soul but could no more pull Edgecombe out of the mire into which Lucien has plunged it than he could read a page of Livy. Lucien is dismembering Edgecombe. I intend to put a stop to that. And I intend to ensure that his heir is my ward."

He smiled, but it had none of the pleasant quality of his earlier smiles. "I shall thus have twenty-one years to put Edgecombe back together again . . . to repair the damage Lucien has done—as much as anything, I believe, to spite me."

"Why can't your cousin find his own wife?" she asked, staring incredulously.

"Well, he might find it difficult," the duke said, turning his signet ring on his finger with a considering air. "Lucien is not a pleasant man. No ordinary female of the right breeding would choose to wed him."

Juliana wondered if she was going mad. At the very least, she had clearly stumbled among lunatics.

"You . . . you want a *brood mare*!" she exclaimed. "You would blackmail me into yielding my body as a vehicle for your cousin's progeny, because no self-respecting woman would take on the job! You're . . . you're treating me like a bitch to be put to a stud."

Tarquin frowned. "Your choice of words is a trifle inelegant, my dear. I'm offering a marriage that comes with a title and what remains of a substantial fortune. My cousin doesn't have long to live, hence the urgency of the matter. However, I'm certain you'll be released from his admittedly undesirable company within a twelvemonth. I'll ensure, of course, that you're well looked after in your widowhood. And, of course, not a word of your unfortunate history will be passed on."

He sipped his wine. When she still gazed at him dumbstruck, he continued: "Your secret will be buried with myself and the Dennisons. No one will ever connect Lady Edgecombe with Juliana . . . whoever you were." His hand moved through the air in a careless gesture. "You will be safe, prosperous, and set up for life."

Juliana drained her champagne glass. Then she threw the glass into the fireplace. Her face was bloodless, her eyes jade stones, her voice low and bitter as aloes. "And to gain such safety . . . such rewards . . . I must simply bear the child of an undesirable invalid with one foot in the—"

"Not precisely." The duke held up one hand, arresting her in midsentence. "You will not bear Lucien's child, my dear Juliana, you will bear mine."

THE ENGAGEMENT
by Suzanne Robinson

*Lady Georgiana Marshal is thrilled at her engagement to
the frail, elderly Earl of Threshfield: in no time she'll be a
widow, free to control her fortune and her dreams. That is,
until her carefully ordered life is sent spinning by the arrival of a brusque gunslinger, a man Georgiana's brother
has sent to scare her away from her plan—and back to her
father's house. But her brother's intentions backfire when
the beauty refuses to be bullied and the dangerously attrac-
tive visitor finds himself falling in love. . . .*

Georgiana raised her chin a bit higher and narrowed
her eyes as the stranger approached. He was almost as
tall as his giant of a horse, lean, as if he'd worked hard
and eaten little. He swept off his wide-brimmed hat
to reveal long, shaggy chestnut hair streaked with
sun-bleached amber. He swept back his long coat behind a gun belt slung low on his hips. High-heeled
boots crunched gravel, and he stuck a thumb in his
gun belt as he reached her. She felt a twinge of recognition, not for the man, but because of Jocelin's description of American frontier garb.

She opened her mouth to inquire if the man had
come from her brother, but he was too quick for her.
A dark blue gaze inspected her as if she were a succu-
lent dessert. Then he appeared to recognize her. His
eyes crinkled, not in amusement, but in irritation.

"Well, if it ain't old George. I been looking all over creation for you. Your danged pa wouldn't tell me where you'd gone. Well, come on, girl. Time to pack up and swim."

Georgiana drew her brows together, straightened her shoulders and said, "I beg your pardon?"

"I reckon you should."

His lips curled in a grin that was at once contemptuous and appreciative. Georgiana wasn't the daughter of a duke for nothing. Giving this barbarian a chilly nod, she turned on her heel and spoke to the Threshfield butler, who had come out of the house upon the arrival of the stranger.

"Randall, send this person on his way."

"Yes, my lady."

"Hold on a minute."

Georgiana paused in her progress around the wagon. "You appear to be looking for someone named George, sir. There is no one by that name at Threshfield."

A gloved hand settled on the revolver at the stranger's side. Georgiana kept her features fixed in an expressionless mask that hid her uneasiness. This man spoke in a slow drawl like the one Jocelin returned with from America, only the stranger's voice was as rough as his speech, low, throaty, and tinged with a knowing familiarity that bordered on an intrusive liberty.

"Look here, George, Jocelin sent me to fetch you, and I'm going to fetch you, so pack your duds and let's ride."

She had been certain she didn't know him. He was sun-brown, sweaty, and stubbled with two days' worth of beard. His shirt was open, and she could see his chest. His chest! No gentleman revealed his chest to a lady. But he'd called her George again, and that twinge of recognition returned. Once, years ago, a man had called her George. It had been that elegantly savage protégé of her brother's, the one whose presence turned her father's complexion vermilion.

Georgiana studied the blue eyes tinged with sapphire, the wide shoulders. Through the chestnut stubble she could discern the shallow indentation in the middle of his chin. She let out her breath in a gasp. "Dear me, it's Mr. Ross!"

" 'Course it's me."

"Mr. Ross," Georgiana repeated witlessly. Then she regained her composure. He was forcing her to discuss her private affairs before servants, but she wasn't going to let him in the house or talk to him alone. "I knew my brother would be concerned. I've written him a letter he's no doubt received by now, so you've come all this way for nothing. I'm sorry for it, but Jocelin does tend to be high-handed. I'm not going anywhere, especially with a mere acquaintance. Good day to you, Mr. Ross."

She turned her back to him. There was an unfamiliar sound of metal against leather, then a click. Georgiana stopped. One of the laborers swore. Darting a glance over her shoulder, she looked at the barrel of a long-nosed revolver. Her gaze lifted to his casual one. A snake's stare had more feeling in it.

"Now don't get your petticoats in a twist. Jos said you'd be stubborn, and that I was to be patient, but I been clear across a continent and an ocean, and I got no use for spoiled, blue-blooded misses. Jos is laid up, and it's plain infernal meanness to worry him like you done. So I reckon I'll just have to take you back to Texas and let Jos see for himself that you ain't hitched yourself to old Threshfield."

NIGHT MOVES
by Sandra Canfield

"Sandra Canfield's superb style of writing proves her to be an author extraordinaire."
—*Affaire de Coeur*

With the critically acclaimed style readers love, Sandra Canfield delivers a spellbinding mix of bittersweet emotions and intricate suspense in this story of star-crossed lovers forced apart by a vicious betrayal. Years later, Gray Bannon receives the heart-stopping news that the daughter he didn't know existed has been kidnapped. Now, he must return to Christine Lowell's world . . . and the memories of a past he has denied for so long.

"Would you like to see a photograph of Amanda?"

"Yeah."

Christine stepped from the window and across the room to a grand piano whose top was covered by elegantly framed photographs. She selected one and started back toward Gray. Once again by his side, she bent to turn on a lamp. Light swallowed the darkness, illuminating Christine's face. There he saw fatigue and fear, and something much more. He saw the past.

In a split second, a thousand memories came charging toward him, memories that he'd fought to keep at bay. Now he remembered his first realization that the awkward child with the mismatched features had grown into a beautiful woman. He could see her hair, kissed by the sun, floating about her shoulders. He could see her eyes, a luminous gray that could steal a man's breath and leave him pleased with the loss. He'd thought then that someday some man would lose himself completely in their depths; he just hadn't known that he'd be that man. And then, with a shocking rapidity, he saw her standing before him in the hothouse—the same sun-heated hair, her thief-gray eyes now filled with need, her voice sexy and seductive. This was the one memory he avoided like the plague, for that day he had learned a truth that would haunt him for the whole of his life.

"This is the most recent photograph," Christine said. "It was taken a couple of months ago."

Gray traveled the countless miles from past to present and took the photograph. The moment he viewed it, all other thoughts, all memories, fled from his mind. He was too busy feeling, although the truth was that he wasn't quite certain what he felt. A sense of unreality, without question. He had fathered this child and yet she didn't seem a part of him, perhaps because she looked nothing like him. Familiar stranger. She looked like, and felt like, a familiar stranger. Perhaps in an attempt to make the unreal more real, he drew his fingertip across the image of this child—across hair as black as a raven's wing, across a smile that lay somewhere between sweet and devilish, across eyes that, like another pair of gray eyes, seemed to see right through him.

"She looks like you." Gray didn't know what else to say as he stood in stunned awe.

"Yes," Christine answered, wondering if he'd be the slightest bit interested in knowing how her prayers had vacillated all the while she'd been pregnant, vacillated between hoping that this child wouldn't look like him and hoping that she would. In the first prayer lay her safety, in the second lay her heart. Part of her would have risked anything to have a startling reminder of what she'd lost. No, she decided, Gray would care nothing about her suffering, and so she repeated simply, "Yes, she looks like me."

SWEET LOVE, SURVIVE
by **Susan Johnson**

"One of the best!"—*Romantic Times*

Back in print at long last, this powerful tale of forbidden passion delivers the memorable conclusion to the bestselling Kuzan Dynasty series begun in SEIZED BY LOVE and LOVE STORM. Only the mistress of the erotic historical romance could bring such fierce sensuality to the reckless liaison between Countess Kitty Radachek and Captain Apollo Kuzan, a liaison that holds their hearts captive in the midst of a nation's upheaval.

In the shadowy glow of the small brass bedside lamp Kitty saw a man sprawled facedown on her pristine white coverlet. A tunic jacket lay in a heap on her carpet, along with a glistening cartridge belt, holster, and sword strap. The officer slept with his face buried in the pillow, clad in a shirt, elkskin breeches, boots, and spurs. His tall, powerfully muscled body, revealed so blatantly beneath close-fitting elkskin and white silk, took up a great deal of space on the birchwood bed. Although most of his face was concealed in the pillow, the long, sun-streaked hair and the portion of dark, winged brow and stark cheekbone verified the usurper as Prince Apollo Kuzan, one of her husband's young captains. Kitty glanced quickly around the bedroom, half expecting to find Karaim and Sahin hovering in the shadows, but Apollo was alone.

It looked as if she'd be sleeping in another bedroom tonight, Kitty rapidly decided. The prince was much too large for her to move, and it was senseless to wake him simply to ask him to transfer to another room. The cavalry troop would still be at Zadia's in the morning. Apollo could rejoin his companions after a good night's rest. However, consideration for the delicate, embroidered counterpane Apollo was lying on induced Kitty to conclude that pulling off his boots before she left might be wise. Those wicked spurs would wreak havoc with the padded silk if he tossed and turned during the night.

One moment Kitty's hands were grasping a grimy cavalry boot, and the following moment she was lying on her back in the center of the bed, her hips straddled by muscular, leather-clad thighs. A lifetime of training in the Caucasus Mountains, as well as the last few years of war, had instilled a finely tuned sense of survival in Apollo. He was a *very* light sleeper.

"Ah-h-h." He relaxed the harsh grip of his fingers around Kitty's slender throat and smiled warmly at the soft female beneath him. No enemy. The adrenaline ceased its furious pumping through his nervous system. "Forgive me, *dushka*," he said, exhaling softly, soothing the angry red marks his fingers had left. The lean, brown hands massaged her neck lightly with apologetic caresses.

Apollo looked down on the beautifully perfumed woman lying under him, felt a fleshy female body between his legs, and the familiar scene stimulated reflexes schooled to perfect response by countless incidents in the past. To wake after drinking and find a woman in bed with him was no novelty—and his need for a woman's warmth was achingly real after weeks of campaigning in the unpopulated steppes.

Without a word he bent to kiss her, not a gentle caress, but a barbaric kiss that shook Kitty's spine, a dangerous kiss that ate at her lips, her tongue; teased the soft interior of her mouth; suffocated the cry of alarm which died in her throat. His hands moved up swiftly, lost themselves in her golden tresses, and held her captive as he lowered his body. Kitty couldn't move, couldn't cry out; she was trapped beneath Apollo's powerful frame while he savored her mouth with a greedy, sharp-set passion—savored her with the avid hunger of two weeks' abstinence, his lips warm and soft, his tongue languidly probing, his sensitive hands leaving their indelible imprint, until a small flame of response, unwonted and disturbing, began to smolder in Kitty. Apollo felt it, the infinitesimal acquiescence, and he lifted his mouth to trace a path downward, lowering his head to kiss the crest of a pale, rounded breast.

Catching her breath, she frantically whispered, "Apollo! Please! I implore you!" But her agitated request was strangely breathy.

Raising his head, Apollo smiled teasingly and laughed again. "You needn't beg, little Marousia. I'm more than willing."

Kitty was seized with both outrage and a terrible excitement. What was he talking about? Who was Marousia? Kitty nervously searched the amused face so close to hers and looked into half-closed, tawny eyes; eyes strangely opaque, dimmed by alcohol. She realized with a sinking feeling that Apollo didn't know who she was. Good God, he didn't know!

On sale in June

MISCHIEF
by Amanda Quick

RAVEN AND THE COWBOY
by Sandra Chastain

THE MAGIC
by Juliana Garnett

*To enter the sweepstakes outlined below, you must respond by the date specified and
follow all entry instructions published elsewhere in this offer.*

DREAM COME TRUE SWEEPSTAKES

Sweepstakes begins 9/1/94, ends 1/15/96. To qualify for the Early Bird Prize, entry must be received by the date specified elsewhere in this offer. Winners will be selected in random drawings on 2/29/96 by an independent judging organization whose decisions are final. Early Bird winner will be selected in a separate drawing from among all qualifying entries.

Odds of winning determined by total number of entries received. Distribution not to exceed 300 million.

Estimated maximum retail value of prizes: Grand (1) $25,000 (cash alternative $20,000); First (1) $2,000; Second (1) $750; Third (50) $75; Fourth (1,000) $50; Early Bird (1) $5,000. Total prize value: $86,500.

Automobile and travel trailer must be picked up at a local dealer; all other merchandise prizes will be shipped to winners. Awarding of any prize to a minor will require written permission of parent/guardian. If a trip prize is won by a minor, s/he must be accompanied by parent/legal guardian. Trip prizes subject to availability and must be completed within 12 months of date awarded. Blackout dates may apply. Early Bird trip is on a space available basis and does not include port charges, gratuities, optional shore excursions and onboard personal purchases. Prizes are not transferable or redeemable for cash except as specified. No substitution for prizes except as necessary due to unavailability. Travel trailer and/or automobile license and registration fees are winners' responsibility as are any other incidental expenses not specified herein.

Early Bird Prize may not be offered in some presentations of this sweepstakes. Grand through third prize winners will have the option of selecting any prize offered at level won. All prizes will be awarded. Drawing will be held at 204 Center Square Road, Bridgeport, NJ 08014. Winners need not be present. For winners list (available in June, 1996), send a self-addressed, stamped envelope by 1/15/96 to: Dream Come True Winners, P.O. Box 572, Gibbstown, NJ 08027.

THE FOLLOWING APPLIES TO THE SWEEPSTAKES ABOVE:

No purchase necessary. No photocopied or mechanically reproduced entries will be accepted. Not responsible for lost, late, misdirected, damaged, incomplete, illegible, or postage-die mail. Entries become the property of sponsors and will not be returned.

Winner(s) will be notified by mail. Winner(s) may be required to sign and return an affidavit of eligibility/release within 14 days of date on notification or an alternate may be selected. Except where prohibited by law, entry constitutes permission to use of winners' names, hometowns, and likenesses for publicity without additional compensation. Void where prohibited or restricted. All federal, state, provincial, and local laws and regulations apply.

All prize values are in U.S. currency. Presentation of prizes may vary; values at a given prize level will be approximately the same. All taxes are winners' responsibility.

Canadian residents, in order to win, must first correctly answer a time-limited skill testing question administered by mail. Any litigation regarding the conduct and awarding of a prize in this publicity contest by a resident of the province of Quebec may be submitted to the Regie des loteries et courses du Quebec.

Sweepstakes is open to legal residents of the U.S., Canada, and Europe (in those areas where made available) who have received this offer.

Sweepstakes in sponsored by Ventura Associates, 1211 Avenue of the Americas, New York, NY 10036 and presented by independent businesses. Employees of these, their advertising agencies and promotional companies involved in this promotion, and their immediate families, agents, successors, and assignees shall be ineligible to participate in the promotion and shall not be eligible for any prizes covered herein.   SWP 3/95

DON'T MISS THESE FABULOUS
BANTAM WOMEN'S FICTION TITLES

On Sale in May

From Jane Feather, nationally bestselling author of
Violet *and* Vanity, *comes a sinful new romance*

VICE

Juliana drew the line at becoming a harlot. After all, she had already begun the week as a bride, and ended it as a murderess. But now she's at the mercy of a powerful, handsome Duke . . . and in no position to bargain. ___57249-0 $5.99/$7.99 in Canada

THE ENGAGEMENT
by beguiling bestseller Suzanne Robinson

An enticing Victorian tale of passion and intrigue that pits the daughter of a duke against a handsome stranger—a man who's part cowboy, part hero, and part thief . . . but altogether irresistible. ___56346-7 $5.50/$7.50

NIGHT MOVES
by award-winning Sandra Canfield

"A master storyteller of stunning intensity." —Romantic Times

With a spellbinding mixture of passion and suspense, past lovers struggle to find a daughter who has been kidnapped . . . and the courage to reclaim love. ___57433-7 $5.99/$7.99

SWEET LOVE, SURVIVE
by Susan Johnson

"A queen of erotic romance." —Romantic Times

In this powerful finale to the bestselling Kuzan Dynasty series begun in *Seized by Love* and *Love Storm*, a man and a woman find themselves in a desperate and passionate liaison, while the fires of a nation in revolution burn around them. ___56329-7 $5.99/$7.99

Ask for these books at your local bookstore or use this page to order.

Please send me the books I have checked above. I am enclosing $___ (add $2.50 to cover postage and handling). Send check or money order, no cash or C.O.D.'s, please.

Name _____

Address _____

City/State/Zip _____

Send order to: Bantam Books, Dept. FN159, 2451 S. Wolf Rd., Des Plaines, IL 60018
Allow four to six weeks for delivery.

Prices and availability subject to change without notice. FN 159 5/96